H O' M, O

HENRY O'MALLEY, OMEGA

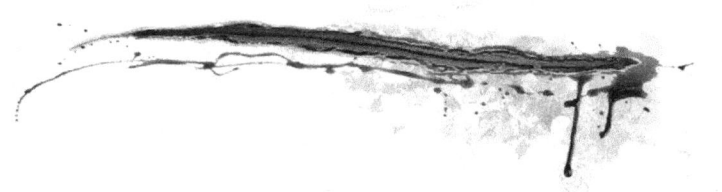

a sparrows hollow lycanthropic adventure

SA Collins

HO'M,O — Henry O'Malley, Omega

A Sparrows Hollow Lycanthropic Adventure

Date of Original Publication: 01 January 2015

ISBN 13: 978-0692391488

ISBN: 0692391487

Acknowledgements —

This was written in part as a NaNoWriMo* 2014 Writer Challenge. It was awarded as a Winner of the challenge on November 26, 2014. Please look into and support this very worthwhile organization and the NaNoWriMo events in your area at www.nanowrimo.org.

- NaNoWriMo - National Novel Writing Month (held in November of each year).

Dedication

For Michael, one of my early champions and a champion of men and werewolves. Mike, this book is for you. You have been a solid friend, a thoughtful and considerate critic — providing a careful eye to my men and the worlds they inhabit. I trust you and your views very nearly as if they were my own. I'll always see you running with my wolves of Sparrows Hollow. You're one of the pack now ... *go git 'em boy!*

— *S.A. Collins*

Special thanks to out country artist **Steve Grand** (stevegrand.com) for providing a well-spring of inspiration (as well as encouragement) for my wolves of Sparrows Hollow. I am indebted to his generosity of spirit and sense of brotherly love.

"This here is fluff, plain and simple" — as my Hank would say. Slightly scary and *erotically* charged fluff, but fluff, nonetheless.

But having grown up just after the classic era of Hollywood monsters, my exposure to them was from the afternoon movies the local TV station would run that I watched when I got home from school.

I've always liked classic horror monsters. To be clear, I am not talking the slasher films of the 70s and 80s which were all the rage when I was a kid. No, I am speaking of the classic golden era of horror film making. You know, the likes of Dracula, The Wolfman, The Mummy, those classic horror monsters from our collective past, brought to life by such wonderful character actors as Lon Cheney Jr., Bela Lugosi, Boris Karloff, and Christopher Lee. Those men of that era still do it for me. Even now when I catch one on DVD, or streaming from one of the online services, I become a kid all over again.

It's one of the reasons I love the new show *Penny Dreadful* on cable television. All the classic gothic monsters in one ensemble cast. What could be better? And there's another element from that show that I particularly like — the slow reveal of who and what they are and how they came to be. There is brilliant writing going on there. As a writer myself, that is a sure-fire way to gain my attention. I've re-watched those initial episodes over and over again because I can't wait for those monsters to engage me again. And it is that sentimentality that the creators of that show imbue into those storylines that has me hungry for more. I love how the writers are doing that — preying upon your heartstrings for these beloved characters of classic gothic literature.

But as I said, I grew up just after the whole era of the serial movies that used to play before the main picture was run. But I have attended several retrospective showings where I got to see them in action on the silver screen. It's lovely that you can watch them at will in your own home, but nothing beats seeing Lugosi some thirty feet tall on the silver screen, as he was intended to be seen. I was always sort of jealous (or *jelly* as the kids say nowadays) that I wasn't a kid from that era. How *magical* it all would've seemed.

So when I decided to write about them I thought I'd put a slightly more adult spin on them but set them in that era of the classic horror movies - the 1940s and 50s, an era where things were simpler, where we weren't so attached to gadgetry and technology. We were still sort of discovering what technology could do for us as a society. It was a far more innocent age, an age where magic still had a mystery to it, a thread of fear that would linger in the air.

To be honest, I wanted tech out of the way. I wanted to concentrate on what intrigued me most, the singular selling point of those stories: *the characters*. Thus my boys of Sparrows Hollow are set in a rural part of the Appalachian Mountains in West Virginia.

I wrote this to put a gay spin on the classic werewolves genre. I've read quite a bit of M/M romance works where the shifter genre has taken off with gusto. I thought I could take a werewolf storyline and and see how I could put my own spin on it. It was intriguing to see what would come of it.

It was also my NaNoWriMo challenge story for 2014 and I won the challenge and completed the bulk of what you have here during that month of writing. I also chose the topic as one of my very first fans is a big time werewolf fanatic; I wanted to do something for him, as well.

But I wanted these stories to be short and episodic in nature, ending each with a great big Happy For Now (HFN) moment but with a thread of — watch out, *all is not as well as it seems* feel to them. The whole "stay tuned" or "until next time …" element, you know?

So this is my effort to give my readers that whole silver-screen serial flick of yesteryear but with a big ol' gay and slightly *erotic* twist. My boys do love the man-on-man action in this tale. Forewarned is forearmed, and all of that.

This work, as with the majority of my works, is a character study. It is far more important to me that you come away with a greater understanding of who the character is, rather the situation they are in. I want you to know these men intimately. They will break tropes; they will break momentum. All of it is intentional. Because the mind in literature is the one seldom written about with all of its foibles and follies – the desire to mentally walk over something again and again. In the case of Hank and his boys, it is the war between monster and man. That is the true nature of this work. But a little sex along the way won't hurt things either, hmmm? After all, it is what keeps them rooted to their humanity in the midst of all the horror their inner-monster can bring.

As this work is episodic in nature, it does not attempt to wrap everything up in a tidy bow. It will hopefully provide just as many questions as it attempts to answer. So just sit back and let my boys wash over you. I hope you enjoy my boys of Sparrows Hollow. They've become my favorite classic monsters now, infecting me with their salacious and horrific ways. I hope you'll find them infectious too.

Until next time…

-SA C

CHAPTER ONE

Riley Raintree

I guess the best way to begin is by telling ya who I am. Yeah, that'd be good, I guess.

My name is Henry O'Malley, but most people around here call me Hank. I was named after my daddy, but he ain't around no more. Not that he left us or nothing. Well, not by choice. See, my mama got pregnant with me a few years before Daddy joined up to the army. This happened shortly after Pearl Harbor at the start of our part in the Second World War. I guess the government got desperate. Not that my dad was in poor shape or nothing. From the pictures I'd seen of him, and the man I know'd he'd become before he shipped off, I spied that he was a mountain of a guy — massive, monumental enough to rival Hercules hisself. The only reason he flew under the radar for most of the draft I guess was because we were in a Podunk of a town in the furthest backwater you could find. And you'd still have to walk a couple of miles further to get here — even then, you still might get lost, the kind of place that was so far off the beaten path that you'd have to pipe sunshine in, as we'd like to say.

Sparrows Hollow wasn't the kind of town that appeared on any map. Just 'twasn't worth the trouble. I think the last census had us pegged at about 500 people who called her home. I was surprised by that because I swear you could walk for miles and never see a single soul and you wouldn't have to try too hard to do that, neither.

But as I said, it was just Mama and me now. Daddy wasn't in the picture on account of him going off to the war and they sorta lost him, no body to bury; no funeral to hold — only because we never knew what happened.

'Twasn't like the only time Daddy'd left us, neither. While he and Mama got along for the most part, they did have *discussions* about things I wasn't a part of. Daddy'd go off for a couple of nights a month. He'd never say where he'd gone or what he'd done. Didn't make Mama happy none, but he was the man of the house so no one did anything to stop him. 'Twas the was the way 'twas, thassall.

I remember one time when Mama accused him of having another woman in his life in some other town. He told her that there wasn't any woman and that he had to take care of business on those nights a couple of counties over with some of the boys. A guy thing. But he swore *"'twerent any women involved."* I don't know how he convinced her, or what he said, but somehow she believed him. Didn't make it any easier on them or me, but we learned to accept it.

Then came the call from the war; he went and just never came back. Yet, there were times I swear I could feel him near: while I was walking home from school, or when I was out tryin' like hell to catch some fish in the one creek we'd used to fish in that I could guarantee hadn't been ruined by the mines. It wasn't that I heard him, just a familiar scent on the air, something that was intrinsically him — from memory, deeply rooted inside of me since I was a boy. I never knew what to make of it. Mama said it was just his spirit watching over me.

We did okay because along with Daddy's pension from the Army, Mama had inherited the general store from her father when he passed. So at the very least we had food and a roof over our head. To make things a tad easier, Mama took to selling the house we had and we took to living in the small apartment above the store. Doing so, we were able to eke out a decent life.

For a few years it went like that. It was just Mama and me. We did the best we could. It meant that I had to grow up quite a bit faster than most of my friends. What few I had. There was little time for playtime or just being a kid. It was a life filled with school, the store and just generally getting along as best we could.

That's when Cora Reiff entered our lives. Cory, as I'd come to call her, was as gentle a soul as you'd ever meet. She was of an average height, but had the appearance of a farm woman of German stock. Though she had probably had the coloring of an Aryan for most of her life, by the time she came to us her hair had lost any of its original hues in favor of a crown of white. Her eyes flashed with a brilliant blue that rivaled the skies and held a spark that belied her age. She was what you called an old soul, a learned soul. She was not book smart in that way that some people liked to profess, but I learned very quickly that she was a walking encyclopedia of life experience that she'd spoil me by letting me plunder whenever the mood struck. It struck quite often, I can tell you that.

Cory and I were like two peas in a pod in the store. Cory didn't have much of anywhere to go, no family to speak of. She just showed up one day to find work. We had some and she charmed the pants off of me, literally, 'cause she said they needed cleaning something fierce. I was eight at the time and I was smitten with the attention she lavished on me that never failed to make us smile. Cory was the balance in my home life, mostly 'cause Mama was not always what they'd call *en pointe,* as she'd like to say. It was a phrase she picked up from her days in college that Cory and me had acquired.

Mama had her good days, that was unless, of course, she had one of her quiet spells. Then Cory and I had to pull more than both our weights around the store to get things covered. 'Twasn't Mama's fault exactly; she just was given to severe bouts of depression over what she said was our miserable lives.

I didn't think they were *so* miserable. Well, they had their ups and downs just like any other. But we did okay. I was a good student in school, well by Sparrows standards, that is. Not that I'd had to worry about going to college or nothing no matter how smart I was. It just wasn't gonna be in the cards for me — no matter how many times Mama had said that was her biggest wish for me. She wanted me to get out and get as far away from Sparrows as I could get. She had her reasons, I suppose. It was just the way life in Appalachia was. There were very few souls that ever escaped her mountains for greener and greater horizons.

But 'tweren't what separated me from the others in town.

You see, I wasn't like the other boys so much. My eyes would rove where they probably shouldn't. Not that I made a big deal about it. I was careful. I mean, I wasn't whatcha'd call a priss or what the boys liked to call a flit. Ya know, as queer as a three dollar bill? And it wasn't that I was light in the loafers or nothing as the other boys liked to say. From all outward appearances I looked rather normal. Average, even, I guess. I wasn't even overly scrawny – lugging around bags of oats and other produce tended to bulk up a guy. But my eye did rove; and it was the boys what held my interest. But I wasn't one of those boys that people whispered about being *that way.* Mostly, 'cause I kept it all to myself.

Still 'twere a few who suspected — for I was no great actor, so some of them 'tweren't fooled none. Not that I did anything to outwardly suggest it, which is why it plagued upon me something fierce – almost to distraction sometimes – on how they coulda known. But 'tweren't because of my size or my manner, I can tell ya that. I was just a nice kid. That's what everyone said.

Nice, nice, nice.

Yeah, well, nice boys got picked on.

Nice boys was watched; that's how that worked.

But I couldn't help myself – being nice was part of who I am. No matter how hard someone's day was, after talking to me at the shop or on the street, they always said I'd put 'em in a better mood on account I was just so danged *nice.* Yeah, I've learned to despise that word, too. I only repeated it so much so you get a feeling of how often I hear that word. I hated it. Not for what it meant, but because I heard it coming my way all the time.

Annoying didn't begin to cover it.

Sure, I had girls who liked me fine. Several of them said I was handsome and had a real nice body, their eyes so wide as they took me in. Some of them tried to press their bodies firmly against mine. I wasn't so sure about that. Cory'd just shake her head and tell me not to fret too much about it, it'd come in my own good time. More often than not, I just ran away from them. I just felt so inferior whenever they paid me any attention.

Mama just said I took after my daddy – yeah, whatever *that* meant – that girls just couldn't help themselves about feeling towards me in that way. Like my daddy, I just brought that out in girls. It still felt strange and awkward when it happened, and it happened far more than I liked.

Though, I guess I could see why girls liked me and all. Mostly 'cause I just let them get away with what they wanted from me. I didn't know how to deal with it all other than run away. As I said before, more often than not, that's what usually happened. I'd've liked to be one of the cool guys, but I didn't think I quite measured up. I came to that conclusion because while I had some solid muscle, I was still a few inches shorter than the other guys at my school. Not puny but just not as monumentally tall like *the pack* was, though for the most part I just tried like hell to get along.

You see, like I said, no one gets away from here much so I'd grown up here with the same kids my whole life. Though the Hollow had its own elementary and middle school, the upper grades congregated a town over in Cavanagh Gap. The Cavanagh Gap Regional High School was home to nearly four hundred ninth through twelfth graders from the four towns that surrounded The Gap, with Sparrows being just one of them.

I liked my high school for the most part. They had good teachers and a decent principal. Well, he was decent for the most part. He tried to be fair, though he seemed to favor some above the others. He was one of them good ol' boys who tended to look the other way for boys who he knew would grow up to be just like him. 'Twere a few fellas who fell under that banner. And then 'twere the other boys. The bad boys. Every schools got 'em, I suppose. Ours just had a twist on them that gave it an edge.

Cavanagh was home to eight boys who traveled together like some sort of wolf pack. Good ol' boys – though of a different kind, I suppose. It didn't help much that the high school's mascot was a wolf neither. These boys took it to heart. I'd grown up with them my whole life. And for the most part, they were decent enough guys. Well, while I was a kid, that is.

But that all changed when we made the move from the Roosevelt

Elementary and Middle School to The Gap high school. Then the boys I'd come to know and considered friends began to fall way like leaves off a tree in autumn – cast to the wind, to observe them from a distance. I wasn't included in their world any longer. At first it hurt, being ignored by them all. But I got used to it as my world slowly but steadily began to close in upon itself until it was just me.

Yet, by the time I started academic life at Cavanagh, those boys began their reign of terror and intimidation. They went everywhere together. And while I had put on some muscle over the summer from eighth to ninth grade, it was by no means as much as those eight boys.

Maynard Renault, a strapping boy of French-Indian descent was the most likable of the bunch. At nearly six foot three and shoulders as wide as nearly some doorways, he was a strapping brute of a guy who I suspected was protecting a very impressionable and sensitive heart. His rustic-hued skin and darkest blue-black hair that shimmered in the sunlight just gave me thoughts I shouldn't be thinking but did whenever I happen to spy him nearby. But I reckon that soft heart thing was just me putting that on him.

His two best friends in that pack were Dylan Addison and Michael Rumsey. Blonde and blue as the day was long those two were, and nearly as beefy as Maynard. They were likable enough, if you were on their good side. I usually wasn't – though I had Maynard to thank half the time for him pulling them away from me as their favorite chew toy. They was just being boys – even if I'd been the target on more than one occasion.

Then there was the unholy trio: Toby Moynahan, Darby Pembroke, and Spike McGhee. Spike's name wasn't really Spike; it was Raymond. But he made it abundantly clear: you didn't dare call him *anything* but Spike.

From that first day at Cavanagh I'd heard that Raymond had changed his name along with his new tough-as-nails bad boy status to Spike, I couldn't figure out why he'd want a name like that. Only to find out during PE that same day how descriptive the name was. It seemed that Raymond was packing one a helluva spike in his drawers. Come to think of it, the entire pack of boys weren't shortchanged by much when it came to their manly bits. I wasn't any slouch there neither, but I didn't have the need to walk around like the cock of the walk about it.

They did, and how.

These boys were dark and ominous, with their DAs combed neatly and greased back with so much pomade that you could fry up an egg with it. Not that I'd want to mind you, 'cause I wasn't too sure how often their hair was washed. But if there was mischief to be had, you can bet this trio of terror had to have their fingers all over it.

That left the two boys that rounded out this particular Cavanagh wolf pack: Tanner Tallman and Riley Raintree. Riley was definitely alpha with these boys. He was the big guy on campus. No doubt about it. Not so much in stature as it was in how he carried himself. And wherever Riley went, Tanner and the pack weren't too far behind with the majority of the student body parting with their coming advance and leaving a stupefied wonder in their wake. Those two, however, were as thick as thieves, always within inches of each other, whispering and colluding on who was going to be their next target, or so I'd imagined.

As of late, it'd woefully been *me*.

Not that they were direct about it. Riley would never go so far as to sully his hands with actual torment. No, he was wont to delegate such matters to his lackeys. But as I said, they'd roam the halls of Cavanagh like they owned the place. In a very real way, and much to my chagrin, they did.

Girls followed them with wide doe-eyed come hither stares, while boys who *weren't* part of their crew, desperately wanted to be, sometimes to the point of looking with something akin to lust in their eyes for them. It was palpable, almost tangible as these boys moved about the halls and grounds of the school.

The Pack, as you've no doubt come to realize I call them, played for the varsity football team during the autumn and then baseball in the spring. Not that I think the unholy trio of Spike, Toby and Darby were into sports much, that was Riley's call, it seemed. Whatever Riley wanted, the boys did, plain and simple. A lot of what they did was like that. Riley's whim was their command and the like. If they hadn't been a constant thorn in my side, I coulda admired that from afar. The way they cohesively moved about the school: confidence and cockiness; grace with a fair smattering of musky testosterone. You could practically smell it on them, heady and deeply alluring in its own way, an allure what would precede them long before you'd set eye upon them.

In any event, it was the middle of autumn and up to this point the team had been doing fairly well for themselves. Looked like they might actually go out on top this year. In a real way I followed the school football team because if they were happy then they usually were celebrating with their girlfriends and leaving me to myself at the store. So things were coasting along fairly well for me since the start of my senior year. As Halloween approached, changing the leaves from green to a myriad of colors, as Mama liked to say, so did the fortunes of the team.

This didn't bode well for me. It never did.

In fact, three days out from Halloween I was picking up the last of my books from my locker and hastily shoving them into my rucksack to make as quick a getaway as possible.

I had reason to be so quick about it and it all began at lunch.

The trio had been quite aggressive with their torments when all I wanted to do was be left alone to eat my small sandwich and some carrots that'd been cut up for me. Since Mama was having one of her spells, I began to wonder if it had been her to prepare a lunch for me, 'cause that'd be rather remarkable. Though in hindsight that mighta been Cory what took care of it. Either way I was thankful. I didn't want it to go to waste.

I spied their approach out of the corner of my eye, moving with all alacrity if only to succeed in making the kill. I hated these times though there was little for me to do but bear it out. Yet I trembled inside like I always did whenever they circled me – clad in their tight jeans cuffed at the hem, white t-shirts with cotton twill jackets that James Dean woulda wore – they cut an impressive image. With their collars turned up, their cockiness reached me before they did. But Toby, Darby and Spike weren't about to leave me to my little lunch. They were having nothing of it. Spike, as usual, was taking point.

"Whatcha got there, pantywaist?"

Seeing the fear in my face, he pouted his lips and made a make-believe cry, leaping up onto the planter, gripping the branch of the tree like some evil recreation of Puck from *A Mid-Summer's Night Dream*.

"A sammich from your mommy?"

Toby nicked my lunch sack before I could reach for it and tossed it to Spike.

"Ooh, lookie here boys, carrots! And cut up so nice and pretty-like."

I made to snatch the bag outta his hands only to miscalculate and with my over-reach, I slipped from the planter box I had chosen far away from the general lunch area, just to keep out of the sight of the pack. Obviously my little plan hadn't worked out quite as well as I'd hoped.

I collided with the ground, hard; I nearly knocked the wind outta me. I moaned in a fair amount of pain as I pushed forward a bit to pick myself back up. I don't know why I was their favorite chew toy, but it probably had to do with that I was known to them. Familiar. Obviously, with no lunch of their own in sight, they were out roaming the halls seeking out boys like me. Chew toys – dogs with chew toys, that's all I could think of when I saw them. That's what these boys seemed to live for when they weren't wrapped up with trying to bag some girl in the hallway or out by the bleachers.

I had the distinction of being their most coveted. No matter what they were caught up with, if I was within spitting distance then whatever had held their attention before seemed to vanish into thin air. It was as if they didn't need to see me; they could smell me coming on the wind. It was totally unnatural, crazy even. But 'twasn't any other way to explain it. There ain't no way that it could be like that; I was imagining it, I was sure. But even now, with those boys closing in on me, it was like they could sense where I was. Smell it.

I felt Toby and Darby's firm hands on my arms, picking me up and hoisting me back onto the planter. They leaned in, their faces so close that the breaths from their nostrils punctuated upon my skin. Then the strangest thing happened. Each of them leaned in even closer and inhaled deeply on either side of my face, then pulled back, their eyes wild, with what I couldn't begin to say. Whatever it was, it wouldn't bode well for me. It never did.

"Yeah, he's prime, boys," Spike said, his breath buffeting against the skin along the back of my neck in soft puffs, raising the small hairs there.

I hadn't even realized he'd moved in behind me. He inhaled as well, running his nose bare inches from the back of my neck. As if that didn't satisfy, I felt the graze of his tongue, gently along my nape, tasting me. He purred from the sensation. I involuntarily shivered from his tongue's caress. I couldn't help myself and I hated that my body had betrayed me yet again with them.

"Oh yeah, boys. He's prime for the plucking," Spike said.

The other boys glanced knowingly at each other and smiled, darkly. A deep malice percolated there in their eyes. A low guttural growl poured from Spike's throat. I involuntarily shivered from head to toe. I couldn't help it. Riddled with shame over what these boys did to me, I found I couldn't look them in the eye. A hand firmly on my shoulder from Spike brought me out of my shivering stupor. That slap, so sudden that it was jarring, caused me to cough as I'd accidentally inhaled quite a bit of spit in the process.

"Easy, Hank, easy there boy," he cooed softly, rubbing my back with his hand, ever so gentle like.

I sputtered and tried to gather myself. It was a lot harder than I thought. The boys chuckled softly as if they were all sharing a little joke at my expense. Their behavior this time around was far different than they'd ever acted before, almost friendly like. The end result of this was I didn't know how to respond.

Spike moved to the right side of me, plopping his butt down alongside mine; I felt the force of his landing as it shook the planter bench. Toby countered by moving next to Darby. I spied them all slowly. Each of them had a gleeful, dark look as they watched me back. Inside my stomach flipped and for a moment I thought I'd toss up the few bites of my sandwich I was able to take. Spike slinked his arm around my shoulders and pulled me close so the side of my face burned with his breath as he spoke softly to me, dark like, with a brutal coldness to it that would burn enough to make Lucifer hisself proud.

"Now see, we was sent out to find ya, Hank." Spike shook his hand on my shoulder, coaxing me to lean into him the tiniest bit. "It's time. Riley says so."

Darby and Toby nodded just once but their eyes, that dark and pointed stare cutting me. Then it dawned on me what that look was. It was the same one I'd spied on Tanner once when he'd cornered Julie Pinkett out by the bleachers. Lust. That's what that was. Hunger and lust. No mistaking it.

But why me?

Because they know ... That's why. A dark thought slithered to the front of my mind. I couldn't help it.

"'Sokay, buddy. Really. Ain't it boys?"

Toby and Darby just nodded their heads.

"Why sure it is," Spike softly continued.

Toby squatted down in front of me and placed a hand on my knee. "Things have changed, Hank."

"Yeah, you're one of us now," Darby said, then ducked a bit because Spike's hand lifted like was meaning to backhand the guy. Toby just sprung back so he couldn't become a target either. Hell, with his move even I jumped a little.

"Way to speak out of turn, Darb. Keep it in your pants for a bit, will ya?"

Spike's dark stare softened considerably as he turned back to me. He smiled warmly, shaking his arm around my shoulder and he leaned in again.

"Riley says it's just time, time for you to be one of the guys. And you know you ain't gonna disappoint a guy like Riley when he calls ya up, now are ya?"

I was speechless. I mean, while the unholy trio made no bones about making my life a veritable hell from time to time, I wasn't even so sure that Riley had ever taken any real notice of a guy like me. When I hadn't responded in what Spike considered an adequate amount of time, he pressed me to do so, "Well, are ya?"

"A-am- am I, what?" I stuttered.

Toby and Darby just snickered softly at my little flub.

Spike practically growled at them and they were smart enough to look sheepish under his gaze. It seemed even this trio had an alpha amongst them. Then Spike turned his attention back to me.

"Now, listen up Hank. It's all really quite simple. Riley says it's time. So what that means to you is you gotta meet us out at the old Witherspoon place on Halloween. Now, can you do that, Hank? You wouldn't want to disappoint Riley, now would ya?" He shook his arm around me again.

"No," I whispered, and Spike chuckled bringing the side of my face to his lips as he kissed my temple, out in the open and everything! I froze, watching Toby and Darby carefully at Spike's little show of affection.

"That's our boy. Things'll get better now. You'll see, right boys?"

Toby and Darby moved in a bit and each patted me softly.

"Yeah, Hank. It's all gonna work out. No sweat. You'll see."

"Yeah, Hank. Riley's gonna be over the moon that you've agreed. I promise ya that," Darby continued that train of thought.

"Yeah, uh, okay. When?" I turned to Spike who was grinning like that Cheshire Cat from that Alice in Wonderland in that Disney movie that played here a year or so back. It was a welcoming-looking smile that had no small degree of evil mixed in. Hunger. Lust. They were there, too.

"Halloween, at dusk. Don't disappoint him, Hank. You wouldn't like Riley when he's disappointed."

The boys looked away, uncomfortable as if the very thought of a pissed off Riley was one of the worst things that could happen. As if to drive home his point, Spike continued, "And he'd come looking for you. So don't even *think* about hiding out. He'd know where to find you."

Spike ran a finger along the side of his nose — furthering my suspicion on how they were taking this whole sniffing things out to a whole different place.

"I won't; I swear it," I said softly.

The boys and Spike seemed to release a breath they didn't know they were holding in.

"Great. Well, we gotta get. Becky Sue and Bobbie Jo ain't gonna get all hot and bothered if we ain't there to do the rustlin', right boys?"

They both chuckled in their dark shared joke at the girls' expense. I eyed them all with what I knew was a thinly disguised look of worry on my part. To my great surprise, Spike responded by leaning in real close, his eyes carrying none of their darker shades of malice. Only softness radiated there.

"Hey now, we're just blowin' steam, Hank. Don't you worry your pretty head about those girls. They don't mean half as much as you do to us. Just wait. You'll soon see."

He ran a hand along the side of my face while his was a myriad of emotions the likes I never thought I'd see on him. My eyes darted to Toby and Darby, and their expressions were very soft too. They all looked like they were gonna hug me or something — I just didn't know what to think.

"C'mon boys. Let's leave Hank here to his lunch."

Then to me, "You eat up, Hank. And don't you worry about the boys none. You're gonna be one of us. Protected. We care for our own. You'll see."

He stood up and the boys started to move off. I watched them go, each of them turning to watch me sitting there watching them. Dumbfounded, confused and thoroughly upside down with emotions I really didn't have any way to sort out.

In short, I was a complete mess.

So when the end-of-day bell sounded, signaling the close of my last class, I made a mad dash to my locker to gather my things. Thinking of grabbing only what was necessary and with all haste make my way out to my bike and home. I hadn't counted on Riley and Tanner intercepting me half way to my goal.

"*H—a—n—k …* " a voice whispered so soft over the din of the other students' coming and going, a cacophonous rattle of voices and clanging locker doors, that I shouldn't have been able to hear it at all.

But I did… and I trembled, from head to toe I could barely keep my insides from flopping around and collapsing under its weight.

"*H-a-n-k …* " a pull so strong, right from the inside of my chest. My heart raced and was utterly calm all at the same time. I couldn't explain it. I didn't have any idea on how to deal with it.

"*Come to me Hank … I need ya to find me.*"

I didn't know why I knew it was Riley, but I did. I don't think he'd spent no more than five or ten words in my general direction in my entire life. Now he'd just racked a dozen more in the span of only a few seconds. A soft lyrical female voice broke my bewildered trancelike stupor.

"You okay, Hank?" Miss Appleby suddenly appeared to my right, stepping out of the music room and startling me. "My goodness, Hank. You look like you've seen a ghost. Are you feelin' okay, son?"

I nodded, unsure of how I'd sound if I said anything to the contrary. Besides, I didn't know how I'd be able to explain how I was hearing Riley Raintree's voice over everyone else and how it made me go all weak inside like just the thought of going to him did right now.

"*Tell her you're fine, Hank. Come to me and all of it will be fine. I swear it.*"

Like that command alone evened everything out, I regained my composure and ran a hand through my hair, straightening up a bit as I did so.

"I - I'm fine, Miss Appleby. Thank you for your concern. I guess I just felt a bit off for a second or so. I'm fine now."

Her face had only relented the tiniest bit of concern at my response. But she seemed resigned to let it go just the same.

"All right then, but why don't you get on home, just in case you feel like that again. All right? I'd feel a whole lot better if your mama were there to see to you if it came on you again."

"Yes ma'am."

I moved off, hiking my rucksack onto my shoulder with all haste to get outside.

The brilliant autumn sun felt good upon my face as I strode as quickly as my feet would carry me without running like a mad fiend to my bike because I know'd that draw too much attention. It seemed that Riley had other ideas though. As before, his voice seemed to come from all around.

"No, Hank … please … "

The pain buried in his plea gnawed at my insides something fierce. I stopped. I couldn't move. His words alone seemed to guide me.

"You need to come to me. I haven't left school yet. You need to find me. You know you do. It wouldn't go well for you to put me off. I know you feel that."

As if to prove his point a sharp cold thread seemed to slither into my heart and gripped it so hard I nearly doubled over from the sensation. Not exactly painful, but a clear warning of what could happen if I did refuse. The trembling began again, as if I could feel his eyes on me already.

"I feel it too … it hurts. Come to me and I promise I can make it better."

His voice was everywhere and nowhere — all at the same time. Yet, no one but me seemed to take notice.

I stopped suddenly only two or three steps away from my bike. I couldn't explain it but as if a veil had been lifted, I suddenly knew where he was. I knew it as sure as I was standing here looking at my bike and the path to home stretching before me, just beyond my finger tips. But the pull from Riley was so strong. My heart ... he was right; I was hurting.

"Hank. Please ... don't deny me. Don't deny us."

I struggled with one more step. The pull deepened; I gasped. Everyone moved about me completely unaware of the severity of what I was going through. Whatever this was, however it was happening, it was unbearable the more I struggled against it. I burned for Riley, burned in ways I never dreamt possible. This was ludicrous. I didn't even *know* him. Not really. And yet ...

"Hank ... please, make it stop."

I could almost hear him panting. He was in pain and I was the cause.

So I turned, walked past the front of the school. A glance back at my bike still racked up, all by itself now, faded into the distance. There was no one wandering around but myself. The place almost seemed deserted. I moved further onto the school grounds, past the school building toward the stadium. I looked around – no one seemed to be here, so I continued across the football field to the far side where the bleachers ran alongside the forest.

I stopped at the first step that would take me beyond the waist-high fence that separated the football field from the stands themselves. I knew that Riley was on the other side of these bleachers. I knew that as sure as I was breathing, panting, with a mix of trepidation and fear over what would come next. I don't know why I knew my next few steps would change everything in my world, but I did. With each touch of my foot on the ground, a feeling of a corner being turned, a new perspective on life seemed to be opening up to me. It also felt like whatever this was, once done, there'd be no going back.

As if sensing my dilemma, Tanner stepped out from the shadow of the bleachers causing me to take a step back. Seeing this, he softened his stance considerably, making him far more approachable.

"He needs to see you. He knows it's early. But it's been hard for him lately," Tanner said quietly, almost reverently, as he walked toward me, a deep look of concern coloring his face. As he approached me, I recalled what I knew about him – gauging any cause for concern that might arise from our exchange.

Tanner Tallman, was the most appropriately named guy I ever did meet. His name not only fit, because it was descriptive from the moment you saw him – he was a big guy – easily 6'3" or 4", but he was built like a linebacker should be. He was ruggedly handsome with that ruddy tone to his skin like he had some Injin in him but with the most brilliant hazel eyes that sparkled just as bright as they can be, wolf-like eyes – a great catch for some lucky girl, I was sure. I started to move past Tanner, but as I did, he placed a big, though gentle, hand on my shoulder. I froze – not knowing what the hell I was doing or what Tanner was about to do to me. I know my eyes were wide with fear as I looked slowly from his big hand on my shoulder up his massive arm to his gentle face.

"Want me to hold that for you?" he glanced at my rucksack.

I'd forgotten I still had the damned thing on.

"Uh, yeah, sure," I shrugged it off and handed it over to him. "Thanks …"

"Uh-huh. And Hank?"

"Yeah?" I stared, wide-eyed at this upside-down moment I was having with him and not bothering to hide it.

"Go easy on him. Just, uh …" He scratched his head like he was at a loss for words. "Well, do what he says. Ah, hell. You'll see soon enough." He glanced back over his shoulder. "I'll go get your bike for ya. That way you won't make anyone worry about what happened to ya, okay?"

I nodded.

Tanner moved away from me to go gather my bike from the rack out front, leaving me completely alone with the jock god on campus, Riley Raintree. It was like I was having an audience with campus royalty. Nothing short of it.

I slowly, and as quietly as I could, moved along the bleachers, glancing around to make sure that it wasn't some kind of set up by the boys. Everything was so still, an eerie-like stillness. Didn't do my nerves much good, I can tell ya. Given my recent past with them it wasn't a foregone conclusion that I was safe, by any stretch of the imagination.

The thing was, there were absolutely no sounds to be had out here, like the forest itself was holding its collective breath while I made my way back to Riley. This served to only add to my apprehension in this whole mess. As I took each step my mind grappled with the very thought that Riley Raintree wanted to see me. Riley was so beautiful, so unattainable, so, well, everything that a guy can be blessed with. And he was an Injin, too. Not that I had any prejudice toward them. Hell, I wasn't so bold to think I was above it all just 'cause I was white or nothing.

I came up to the corner of the bleachers, a do-or-die moment. I didn't know what to expect. I wasn't even sure why I was really here. All I know'd was that the pull had intensified the closer I got to him, but in a way that was completely calming now. I knew he could feel it too. I didn't know why I thought these things, or why I felt them, even. This whole set of events had completely rewritten my world as I knew it.

I turned the corner and found Riley sitting on an inverted milk crate, his head in his hands, hunched over, very much in pain.

"R- Riley?" I said so softly, afraid I'd startle him.

I spied him sitting there: tight-fitting jeans hugging every inch of his muscular legs, down to his size 12 loafers. He had on a simple white T-shirt that it looked painted on, as if it were ready to bust at the seams. Over this he had a crisp white button-down shirt and the requisite letterman's jacket, bearing the school's red and white colors, that had become as iconic on him as he had become iconic at the school. Riley Raintree was admired by most in the five towns that made up this school district. He was known in all of them.

He looked up, his dark brown eyes wet with tears. Bloodshot. Worry across his handsome face, plain as the day was long. All I could think was I had somehow caused this to happen to him. I didn't know how; I didn't understand it. But every fiber of my soul said that Riley's pain was my own. And just as peculiar, in equal parts, I knew I was the cure and life itself to him. I just knew it. Plain and simple. How or why, well that was beyond my comprehending at this point in time. I wasn't prepared for what Riley had in store for the likes of me.

He launched himself from that crate like he was shot out of a cannon. I didn't have any time to react as he had forcibly pinned me up against the bleacher supports. His mouth was on mine with his hands on either side of my face, ravenously drinking from my mouth as a parched man from a well. At first I was in a dizzying array of feelings and emotions, confusion laced with fear, lust mingling with, dare I even think it, *love? No. That was absurd. I didn't know the guy, not really.* Though for some reason, I didn't seem to want to let that feeling go.

Love? It didn't seem possible, did it?

But drink from me, he did. As he took from me I found I had a well of, well, *something* to give him, like it was coming from the very center of me and it was only for him now, like that kiss would bind me to him forever.

I knew somehow that whatever was going on was right, even though it went against everything I'd ever been told about how life works, how men are supposed to be with one another, how wrong I knew I was with the feelings I'd had all along about the other boys in town. As the kiss deepened, those feelings I'd suppressed all along for Riley Raintree came roiling to the top. My long ago fascination with all things him came at me. Wave after wave of it poured through me as Riley's tongue fully pressed into my mouth and my brain lit up with such color and emotion that I sagged under its power. He felt me stumble beneath him and his arms came around me, keeping me bound to him, pulling me tight against him to where I thought I wouldn't be able to catch my breath. I didn't fight him when he did that. I put him squarely in the driver's seat and I was along for the ride.

I shook, I trembled, I quaked with how strong the emotions were passing between us. In that moment, in that torrential, earth-shattering moment, I knew I belonged to him. I belonged to him in ways that were unthinkable, improbable. Yet here I was clinging to him and kissing him with a ferocity I scarce knew I had in me.

As sudden as it all began he broke the kiss and pushed back a couple of steps, both of us panting as if we'd just run the fastest mile on record. I literally fell on my knees to the ground – winded, breathing hard myself.

"Riley?" I panted between breaths.

Riley turned to me slightly, before he started to walk away. My heart ached something fierce the further he pulled away from me. His straight shoulder-length blue-black hair caught the sun as he stepped away from the bleachers. Riley was a very good looking boy. I knew he was one hundred percent Injin – adopted by the town's doctor – but the darkness from his ruddy smooth skin, to those angled cheekbones and full lips, caught my attention like no other. Mingo they'd said he was. It was thought he didn't know much about his tribal family life having been adopted by the doctor and his wife since he was a very young boy. His adoptive parents were good to him. He seemed happy, though not nearly as happy as when I was in his arms. That kiss told me everything I needed to know about Riley Raintree. I opened my mouth to call to him once more and he stopped before I could form the words in my mouth.

My mouth …

I pursed my lips a little, ran my tongue along the inside; I could still taste him on me. It was like a powerful drug or toxin; somehow that kiss had infected me. It was the only explanation I could come up with. I slowly rose, pulled away from the bleachers and took a step toward him.

"Come with me," he whispered with a slight turn over his shoulder, not bothering to look at me and yet I could hear him plain as day as if he were saying it directly into my ear. I watched as he moved off, past the line where the school grounds ended and the forest began. After a few more steps, to where he nearly disappeared amongst the brush and trees, I felt that pull on the center of my chest, telling me that I needed to do as he asked. Only it wasn't a request. I knew if he said anything to me now, I'd do it, without question or pause. As if to prove that point I found I was already in pursuit, crossing the distance from the bleachers to the tree line within seconds. I was practically chasing him at a flat out run.

Now if you'd never seen the Allegheny or Smokey Mountains then you just didn't know what beauty was. It was like God hisself had drawn a finger on the land and wrinkled it into the rich landscape that I'd come to know and love. These rolling mountains after mountains were home to me. I didn't care what else there was in the world. This part of the world was home, always would be. The forest was a tricky place, especially in these here parts, dense and thick with virgin woods and brush. Tales of hairy dark beasts what the Injin's had legends about still were told and given weight by those who lived here and had reason to believe in them. Tall tales of wolves who walked like men, hunted and called out in the fullness of the moon. Wolfmen. There was even times when I swore I heard them. But that was just tall tales, right? Like in them movie pictures what I saw in the theater. But despite the tales, I just couldn't picture Lon Cheney, Jr. climbing through the forest in these here parts. The forest may be home, but it could be a very intimidating place to be, too. Yeah, chasing Riley into these woods, I suddenly wasn't so sure about what I'd find in there.

I could hear him giggle like a young boy on a wild chase through the forest. At times I could hear him nearby and at others, when I'd only taken a few more strides, he seemed so far off I couldn't sort out exactly where he was. So I'd stop, a light panting to my breath. I was hardly winded from the exertion. I was what Mama had said about her love of Daddy, she had said it was *euphoric*. I knew what that meant now.

"Ri– ..."

Arms slinked around my waist and his breath was hot upon my neck, leaving soft pecks and a small swipe of his tongue searing a trail of fire along the skin there.

He purred, deep and gravel-like in the back of his throat. Sexy. Very, very sexy.

"Mmmm, you taste better than I'd imagined."

I felt him grind up against me, making me weak in the knees again. I tried to turn around to face him. He wasn't having it. His arms tightened around my chest as he burrowed into my neck. I became so overheated from what he was doing to me. I felt the enormity of him pressing into my backside, the thrust of his hips against me, small grunts from his mouth as he did so punctuating against my neck, making it even harder to concentrate enough to say anything. His hands slipped under my shirt and in one slick move he yanked it clear off my head, flinging it into a nearby bush. His fingers went straight to my nipples, twisting them, fingering them hard and rough. The swelling in my pants was automatic.

A whiff of something on the air caught my attention. Familiar, strong. Deeply strong. Reminding me of ...

Before I could finish that thought, a stab, sharp and piercing was at my neck.

A *bite*.

Riley Raintree had bitten me along that part of my neck that stretched out to my right shoulder. I tried to struggle against it but he growled defiantly, squashing any hope I had of breaking free of him. A round of gooseflesh coursed over me. He reached around my waist and undid the top button of my jeans to shuck my pants down while his bite intensified. I tried to cry out but succeeded in only producing a whimper. It hurt; his teeth seared like a white-hot poker, yet somehow I endured it. The heat from the grip of his teeth upon my flesh only succeeded in making me want him more. A second or two later and I realized he had undone his own pants; his cock was pressing for entry on my backside, sliding between the cleft of my ass. The tip of his cock was very slick; I could feel him dripping heavily along the back of my leg. He growled deeply. He curled his hands up along my torso to grip my shoulders and with one very long thrust he burrowed his way into me.

My mind exploded in a burst of color and intensity that I nearly collapsed under the weight of it all. I had nothing to compare it to, no way to rationalize what was happening to me. He was rending me in two. I was being shredded raw and yet, I still held my ground. Then, like a flash of lightning with his next thrust into me, it came to me.

Riley and I was having sex.

I know I should've know'd what was goin' on but having never done it before, I was at a loss on what it was when it happened. But I knew now.

I keened, loudly – a howl from somewhere deep within reverberated and made the trees rattle. My throat burned with that howl. I was on fire. I heard some wildlife scurry away from us. A few more thrusts and I realized that this was more than Riley fucking me. The bite, the way he was holding me, was nothing short of sheer possession. The nails of his hand brought small welts upon my skin. I didn't care, it only succeeded in making me want him more. With each snap of his hips, his cock pressing inside of me in a place I didn't know I had, he was telling me I was his. He leaned me forward so my shoulder came into contact with a nearby tree while he continued to ravage me. I didn't know it could be like this. It burned, and though it hurt, I found I had enormous pleasure from how he continued to claim me. No matter how much it hurt, I couldn't think of asking him to stop. I wanted to be his. I wanted Riley Raintree to own every part of me. His mouth, his teeth never relented their hold on me as we fucked. My back was covered in the spittle and blood from the grip he had on me with his mouth. The grunting became frenzied as I could feel him build. The smell of copper lingered around us. Blood, bone, and musk. We weren't just fucking. He was rutting and giving me all his worth. I gripped the tree, panting with wanting him to bind himself to me. I knew if he finished himself within me I was marked. I would forever be Riley Raintree's bitch. A very deep snarl broke from his lips against my skin, bringing a new round of pleasure in me. A few hard thrusts later, his hands on my hips, holding so tight that I knew I'd have bruises, we both finally found release.

We both howled, a sound unlike any I'd made before. Guttural, fiercely masculine and primal. Ancient, and very, very dark. The air became still. The forest was quiet. Even the nearby stream seemed to slow its pace a spell.

A second or so after, he relented upon my neck, the blood trailing down my chest and back I was sure. He still hadn't extracted himself from me. I felt his forehead on my back.

"Am I yours?" I didn't know why I needed to have him say it, but I did. He needed to say it. He needed to complete whatever it was that we'd just done.

He pulled out and slowly turned me around so I could face him, pressing my back into the tree. His mouth was bloody, covered with *my* blood, and yet somehow I knew that, too, was all right. It didn't make no kind of sense. Everything was cattywampus. Tilted. Off-kilter. Yet, the simple truth of it remained.

Riley and I were connected somehow, weren't we?

He leaned in so his forehead could touch my own, his breath softly billowing against my face.

"No, Hank," he whispered so softly, I could feel the pain in them. "No."

Those simple words sucker-punched me worse than any beating I'd ever gotten. I thought I knew of pain. When he said that, I realized how wrong I was about it all. My heart sank; I felt myself inwardly recoil. I started to pull away to bend down and pick up my pants, ashamed for what I thought this was, for what I'd allowed him to do to me. As I pulled them up and began to redress he grabbed my wrist.

"NO!" he bellowed.

I tried to shake his hand off of me but he was so strong, like a metal vice kinda strong. I couldn't help the tears that were falling from my face. I was so ashamed. I wanted nothing more than to run. Run and run and never come back. Never find peace again. I was so deeply hurt by him, by what we'd done and what I'd allowed myself to think it meant.

"Hank! Listen to me. Hank!" His voice darkened, deepened and vibrated through me. A shrill of sparrows nearby took flight at the loudness of his voice. Then everything went deadly silent.

I stopped, looking down at my feet, though my eyes darted to his exposed cock. I marveled for a moment of how much there was of him, even in that spent state, and how it had all recently fit so well inside of me. He hadn't even bothered to dress himself yet, his pants still pooled around his ankles. It was a bleary vision to behold through the stream of tears that found no end.

His hands came to my face, forcing me to look up into his eyes. His deep, dark eyes. Eyes I could've lost myself in forever and not care that I'd be missed.

"You've got it all wrong."

I nodded, trying once more to pull away. He held me firm.

"Hank! Listen. Please, *baby*. I need you to hear me."

The plea in his voice hurt me even more. That he felt pain, pain that I'd caused, cut me deeply. Then like a tumbler in a lock, something inside of me clicked.

Baby? Now *that* sure as hell got my attention some.

"What I said to you was true. You are *not mine*. I wish on everything I hold dear and true to me that 'twas that way. But 'tain't that way 'tall. This here's the important part, *are you listenin' to me?*"

I waited, trying to figure out if I should give him the benefit of the doubt I was feeling or not. I finally nodded just once. That seemed to satisfy, so he continued.

"I wish I could claim you to be mine. But it don't work that way. Though it makes me happy to think that you want it like that. Over the moon happy, Hank. You have no idea how happy that makes me to hear you say that about me, *about us*. But," he ran his right hand very softly down the side of my face, a lover's caress I'd like to think. "It's me who now belongs to you. That's why I said no."

"But uh, what we just done …"

He nodded, the most beautiful smile I'd ever witness played across his face. Even with his blood-stained lips and teeth, I'd take that smile from him anyhow.

"Yeah, I can see how you'd think 'twas me in control there," he smirked. "But 'tweren't like that. I wish ta God 'twas, but 'tain't how it works. I am *yours*. I will be nothing *but yours*. The guys may think that I am their leader, but really they'll see that we all will belong to you now. I will be exclusive to you for life. I was hopin' it'd be like that. And I think you want me to be like that. Don'tcha?"

I leaned down and he let go of me, not sure what I was gonna do next. I reached for his pants and brought them up and fastened them for him.

"Riley Raintree, are you fixin' ta ask me to marry you?" I said with a quirk to my brow.

He pushed me up against the tree and we kissed for the longest time, smiles breaking out over our lips as we did so. I let my hands move over his hard muscled body as his did over mine, until a soft cough broke the spell.

"Riley …"

Tanner.

"It's gettin' late. The boys need to hunt soon and Hank's mama is gonna be worryin'," he said softly as he approached us handing me my rucksack.

I eyed my shoulder, bloodied to all hell and gone. It was Tanner who approached me then, his manner all soft and caring. He leaned forward. I sorta pulled back and he stopped, unsure of himself. I'd never thought I'd see the like of these boys ever being worried about what I thought.

Riley came up behind me. "He wants to care for you, Hank. It's how it's gonna be now. We belong to you, now. Ya see?"

Tanner moved closer, his nostrils flaring a bit as he did so, taking my scent in. His eyes darted to my wounded shoulder. He motioned to it with his chin, nearly whimpering in soft, warm tones, like a pup to its mama. I just stood still as a mouse while he came closer. I felt his hands move around me to hold onto the expanse of my back; he leaned in and I didn't quite know what to think. I eyed Riley who just nodded once that everything was okay. Tanner sniffed along my shoulder and then placed his tongue upon the wound that Riley left there and began to lap at it, licking it clean, murmuring softly as he did so. It made me a little weak to have these boys that I'd secretly feared and admired being so close to me, tending to me like they were doing.

My shoulder tingled quite a bit as Tanner continued to clean it with his tongue. A few seconds later and he began to pull back, his face so close to my own, a small stain of blood upon his full bottom lip, his hazel eyes wide, the pupils dilated, drinking me in. I inhaled him; I didn't know why, but it seemed the right thing to do. He began to release me and I sensed there was something he was disappointed in how whatever had happened went. My hands went to either side of his face, my eyes searching his own. Then I felt myself lean forward, as if my body knew what to do with him and I kissed him. I felt him blossom inside. I could feel everything he did, tenfold. The kiss went on for a few more seconds before I began to pull away. I watched his face as he backed up and let me stand on my own. His smile so sheepish and warm. Gratitude. That's what I got from him.

Riley leaned forward.

"Now he's getting it," he said to Tanner.

Tanner chuckled warmly and nodded.

"You was right about that, Ry. It's gonna be magical all right."

Tanner stroked the side of my face and sighed.

They got me dressed and off on my bike toward home, watching me as I took my leave of them. I can't say it one way or the other but I swear it felt like they was with me all the way home. It was silly, 'cause I never did see them, though their scent was still strong as if they was right under my nose and all.

By the time I came up to the store I was having a hard time believing any of it had happened at all – with only the absence of Riley within me reminding me that it had. I apologized to Mama about being so late, made up some excuse of why it was so. Don't know whether she believed me or not. Her eyes softened the tiniest bit at my words and whatever she was gonna say slipped away instead and she moved off with a nod what left me feeling awkward and exposed.

There was a certain look from Cory what made me think that my little tale hadn't slipped past her. The focus in her eyes, never going so far as to touch the gentleness of her face, was something that I committed to memory, wondering if I should ask her about it later or not. There wasn't much I hid from Cory.

When I got upstairs and into our bathroom, I pulled off my shirt and looked at that part of my skin where I knew Riley had marked me. Sure enough, there were two incisions that had completely scarred over, as if they were years old and not freshly made. I didn't understand that neither, but they were there nonetheless. I found myself beaming, a sly and knowing look from what I'd done, and walking like I had a cloud underneath me for the rest of the night. Mama thought that my little choo-choo had well and truly gone completely around the bend.

Freshly scrubbed up from the tub, though inwardly still aching a bit from Riley's absence I made my way downstairs; Cory just watched me while I helped prepare supper for us, her sidelong glances making me flush furiously to the point where I nearly asked her why she was looking that way at me. Once or twice I just about did. She'd stop cutting or stirring or whatever she was doing and stare at me, practically goading me to speak my mind and say something about it.

I chickened out every danged time. She'd just turn and shake her head a bit with a little sigh like she was disappointed that I didn't trust what we had to say what was on my mind.

I knew I should.

It's what we were to each other since I was a boy.

I'd say things to Cory that I'd never tell another soul. But I'd fucked Riley Raintree. How the hell was I gonna say something like that to her? How was I gonna tell her I was in love *with a boy*? Jus 'twasn't right, thassall. That's why I can't do it, even if sometimes she'd look at me with what I could only guess was hope that I'd break, that I'd tell her how scared and happy and every other wild feeling I was having about me and him.

But I didn't.

And I think she knew.

Yeah, she knew.

I sure as hell still didn't.

CHAPTER TWO

This Pack of Boys ...

I got up the next morning about an hour before I usually did. 'Twasn't because of what happened with Riley and the boys the day before, though just thinking about it did make me sort of restless.

I got the store in quick order while I heated up some toast and made the morning coffee. I knew Mama'd be down in a bit to check on my morning routine. I got the stock pulled from the delivery truck that came in around five a.m. and was busy putting it in the stock room when I heard her familiar steps coming down the stairs from our small rooms above. I could hear Cory upstairs workin' on getting breakfast made.

"You get that feed moved over to the far corner like we discussed?"

"Yessum," I huffed a bit as I just completed moving the fifty pound bags she was asking about.

"You're a good boy, Hank. Your daddy would be proud a-you," she smiled knowing how that would please me to no end. It did.

I wasn't a mama's boy by any stretch of the imagination. But she was all I had now by way of family, though I supposed that Cory was a big part of that now, too. So we made the most of our relationship and for the most part things went along pretty smoothly. Mama and I didn't argue; we didn't even debate. She said something needed doing and I did it. Plain and simple.

"Hank, you feelin' okay?"

"Yessum. Why'd ya ask?"

She cocked her head to the side a bit, like she was trying to see me in a different light, and then she turned it slightly the other way. I really didn't know what to make of it. It was like she saw a horn or something growing out of my head.

"Somethin' wrong?"

She pouted her lower lip a bit, as if she still couldn't quite put her finger on whatever it was that she saw and said, "Nah, you just seem a bit different, that's all."

I smirked, "Mm-kay, Mama."

And I went back to loading the last of the stock into the back room. Twenty minutes later and I scarfed my now colder-than-ice toast that had soaked up a helluva lot of butter, a host of eggs and sausage that Cory pointed vigorously at on my plate making it clear that I wasn't gonna skip out on eating a full breakfast. I drank my coffee down in two gulps – 'twasn't all that hot anymore neither but I wasn't gonna say a thing to Cory 'bout it. I felt Mama sneak up behind me, I rose from the table and turned to face her. Her eyes sparkled, wet with a sudden rush of something no doubt from the past.

"You sure have grown some, son. You're turning out to be a spittin' image of your daddy. He was a big man, too."

"Mama, you sure *you* ain't feelin' right?" I smiled like I was the cat who made off with the fish, knowing how she was usually tickled when I sassed her a tiny bit.

"Aw, go on now and get ready for school," she said waving a hand at me telling me to scoot so she and Cory could take over with the smaller stocking that was more manageable for them.

Ten minutes later and I was in the basement again getting the water to the right temperature for my morning shower. I peeled off my work shirt and tossed it into the hamper Mama had set up for us in the corner of the shower room. As they slipped into the hamper I made a point to remember to start washing the clothes when I got home from school this afternoon just so Mama wouldn't be so run down by the time dinner had to get started. And I sure as hell didn't want Cory to handle it. She did enough around here as 'twas. Cory would do it too, but I was a big enough boy to pull my own weight around when it came to the cleaning though. Ain't no shirking that need be done on my part, no sir. As the man of the house, I supposed that I coulda left it to them, but it just didn't seem right to do so. I wanted to help, not put more of a burden on them.

Going to school, running the store and our lives took up a lot of time in my day. It didn't leave me much in the way of idleness what with the store and homework and all. As I started to get into the shower, I stopped and peered at my shoulder in the mirror again. I could see where Riley had bitten me. The puncture wounds were still there, faint lines along my milky white skin. It was hard to see them at all from a distance, yet I remember during the whole time I was with Riley in the forest he had gripped me with his teeth rather hard. I just couldn't figure out why everything had healed so danged quickly. And Tanner lappin' at it didn't solve that riddle none, either.

I sat down on the edge of the small wall in the front of the shower stall while the steam from the shower moved along my body like a rich fog. The heat of the water only served to bring my thoughts back to when Riley was fucking me. Truth be told, my hand and my cock had quite a time last night just thinking about how hard he had taken me in that forest. I sorta liked how aggressive he got with me.

And Jesus, if it didn't hurt me so much when he said when it was over that I didn't belong to him; I just about came apart. Having someone like Riley take full possession of you only to feel like you were tossed to the road, like you was nothing at all, was the worst kind of feeling I ever experienced. Well, that's what I thought at first. How could I know what he'd said would affect a guy like me?

"I wish ta God 'twas that way. No, Hank. It's me who belongs to you now."

I just couldn't make myself believe that. 'Cause the truth of it sorta shook my world. Riley Raintree. Riley Raintree and I fucked, and we *liked* it. I was his and he was mine. I had to have heard him wrong about that. There was just no way that I had me Riley Raintree to call my own. I ran a lazy hand to scratch along my left elbow while my thoughts played on about it.

And what about Tanner being mine too? Say nothing of Spike, Toby, Mike, and the others in his pack? He seemed to think they'd all be behind me as well. I just didn't know what to think. If'n you'da told me this was how it was gonna be now, I'da been walking the other direction just 'cause I know'd you were plumb crazy.

"Don't make no kinda sense no how," I murmured.

I stripped the rest of my clothes off and slipped into the shower. The heat from the water was relaxing me but good. As I poured me some shampoo to wash my hair I sorta froze, 'cause it felt like I wasn't alone no more. Can't say rightly how I knew it to be so, but I did. Actually, nothing is as 'twas supposed to be. Topsy-turvy, that's what this was. Still, that feeling like I wasn't alone pressed in upon me.

I pulled the curtain back and looked around. I didn't see or hear nothing except the water and the sounds of the day getting started out the small basement window which I had opened just a crack to let some of the steam out.

Suddenly I shuddered involuntary like, from head to toe. I'd only felt that one other time in my life, when Riley had first called to me yesterday. I still don't know how that had happened. I just never did hear of such a thing.

"H—a—n—k ... " I could not only hear him, but I could feel him, like he was coursing through my body, which was sorta new. But a quick pulse check inside and it definitely felt like I could feel Riley coursing through me.

I froze, not knowing how to act or how to respond. Suddenly there was a pull from the very center of my chest — like he was calling me, speaking right into my heart. I ached from it. Lawdy, did I ever need to be near him just then. It overwhelmed me and I gasped just a little from it. But I knew it was the only thing that would calm that feeling, like he was thrumming his fingers upon my chest. His voice seemed to come at me from all sides and no sides at all.

"Hank, I need you to find me when you get to school. I'll be out by the stadium again. Our meetin' place, 'k?"

I didn't know how to let him know I heard him and all. It was nothing but strangeness piled on by even more strangeness. I didn't think he could hear me and I felt stupid for doing so, but I vocally whispered my reply anyway.

"Okay, uh, be there in a few, 'k?" I said aloud even thought I felt incredibly silly doing so.

I waited, the water moving about my body. Suddenly I felt something like a caress around my chest and neck before it slithered away and I knew he was gone. I finished scrubbing myself up and rinsing off in record time. I had myself cleaned, clothed and polished up my teeth, kissed my ma and Cory, picked up the rucksack and my lunch and was out the door in less than twelve minutes flat.

The roads were nearly clear of any traffic this early. Folks were up, but they just weren't out and about yet. In fact, I was a whole hour early getting to school. What the hell would I do for an hour with Riley? Suddenly I felt rather foolish for busting my behind to get there.

Unless he … ? I pushed it aside cause it was simply too early to be fucking out in the woods. But given the way I could tell Riley's thoughts of me and what we done, I wasn't so sure that was a hard and fast rule no more.

As I barreled along the road toward school, I noted that there was a gentle fog that settled around me in soft curtains, an alternating path of crisp clarity to murkiness that would obscure everything within a few feet in front of me. The morning was cold, but not unseasonably so, a bite to the air as I sailed down the road. The sun still hadn't quite crested over the hills yet. The pre-dawn sky was that pretty pink-orange that never failed to make me smile. Well, at least until today. Today I was a ball of confusion — 'cause I wasn't a virgin no more. I'd finally had sex. Riley'd seen to that.

Riley …

"Hank …," he called again, like he heard me just thinking about him.

The bike ride was close to twenty minutes on a good day coming down hill from where Cavanaugh High was located one town over and up the opposing mountainside. Only I wasn't coming from that direction. In other words, my journey *to* school was always a bit of hike up to where the school sat overlooking the town and therefore took me a tad longer to make.

Now, I don't know if it was on account-a me and Riley doing what we done, but for some reason, the ride up the hill was easy as punch. I didn't necessarily struggle or nothing before, but now it was as if I were taking a leisure stroll. Nary an effort at all.

'Twasn't anyone around on the campus at this early hour, at least not that I could see. I pulled my bike around the side of the school and came to a stop when an absurd thought crossed my mind. It was stupid, ridiculous even, but I found myself doing it anyhow.

I stopped, looked around, just to make sure that no one was there. Thank the Maker, though I think he ultimately didn't have any hand in this whole thing what was happening to me, 'tweren't anyone around to see what I was about to do.

Embarrassed, but thankfully quite alone, I lifted my face up and against my better judgment, and I inhaled, - *deeply*. Among the smells of the morning I found him. Like a loose thread on a throw rug, I pulled upon it – a warm smile coursing across my lips.

Riley.

I don't know how, I couldn't figure out why it was even remotely possible, but that scent was undoubtedly him. I'd know it anywhere. The trouble was, I wasn't so sure how I knew this. Then his words rang again in my ear.

"Yeah, I can see how you'd think that it was me in control there. But 'tweren't like that. I wish ta God 'twas, but 'tain't how it works. I am yours. I will be nothing but yours. The guys may think that I am their leader, but really they'll see that we all will belong to you now. I will be exclusive to you for life. I was hopin' it'd be like that. And I think you want me to be like that. Don'tcha?"

He *belonged* to me …

Impossible, but there he was. His scent.

"Riley?" I whispered.

"Hank … I'm right here, waitin' for ya," his voice lilted in the air like the wind carried it only for my ears.

I slowly walked the bike to the other side of the stadium to where I found Riley yesterday. I stopped on the other side of the track, dropped my rucksack containing my books and my lunch and leaned the bike next to the chain link fence. I followed that scent to locate him though I knew I didn't need to. He was there; I was sure of it. As I came around the back of the bleachers he was standing there, leaning against the framework. A devilish smirk played across his lips, his deep, dark brown eyes so wide and awestruck, like I was some sorta gift he had been expecting all along.

He pulled himself free of the bleacher support and walked slowly to me. In the stillness of the early morning he was stunningly beautiful in that way that only men can be. Well, to my way of thinking, at any rate.

His hands came up to either side of my face, big rough hands like mine, hands that knew of work, and of a life in this town. A man's hands. It was the most wonderful feeling I ever did feel.

He didn't say a word, nor did I. His eyes drank me in, coursing over every inch of my face, memorizing me — like pools of the deepest, darkest chocolate, those eyes were. I watched him silently, finding it so hard to breathe with him so close. 'Twas like my lungs would only find the air about him to their liking. His eyes continued to slowly take in every part of my face, like he wanted to commit it all to memory, in case I faded away or something … *like that was ever gonna happen.* I mean, I wasn't stupid. I had me Riley Raintree; and he was mine. He said so. I wasn't going anywhere that would threaten to take him away from me.

I felt the soft warm pinpricks of light from the sun breaking over the crest of the mountain top. In that deliriously romantic moment, his lips met mine and he kissed me so tenderly, as if he couldn't believe he could do this to me. I swear I'd let him do this to me whenever he wanted no matter what it cost me. I know he said he was mine, I heard the words, but the feeling was mutual. He could have me just about any way he wanted. His tongue lapped at my mouth as he took a step closer. The sun bathed our faces in brilliant sunlight, the fog softening it here and there. There were birds softly tweeting and a twittering in the distance.

It was nothing short of magical.

I felt him start to smile as the kiss deepened until it slowly turned to a soft laugh that billowed in tiny puffs into my mouth. This made me smile too, though I can't say why. It seemed whatever he felt, however deeply he felt it, I felt it too.

Connected.

His right hand slowly slipped from my face and snaked around my waist so his hand could move along my buttocks. He cupped one of my well-muscled ass cheeks roughly in his hand. I grew hard with just that move alone, his eyes never leaving mine.

"Am I still yours?" he asked me so softly I barely heard it.

I nodded slowly, making sure that I didn't break eye contact with him, too afraid to trust my voice.

"If'n you want to still be, that is."

He chuckled softly at that and pulled me tighter to him to where I thought he'd crush the life outta me. He buried his face into the crook of my neck; his breath was hot and scalding against it. He radiated heat like the sun itself.

He could scorch me any day. Least, that's what I wanted to say anyway.

"I still can't believe we done what we did yesterday," he whispered into my neck. I didn't know what to say. I liked it too. A lot, actually. I didn't know how'd he feel if I told him, so I just turned my head and kissed the side of his to let him know as best I could given the circumstances how I felt about it.

"You can have me now, if you want to."

I don't know why I said it. It just came out before I realized it. My eyes went a bit wide at my saying such a thing so early in the morning.

He chuckled again and leaned back so he could watch me.

"As much as I'd like that, the boys might not want that right now."

I pulled back for a second and he let me go, a look of guilt rattling him for saying that.

"The b-boys?"

He ran a nervous hand that until a second or so ago had been manhandling my ass, along his neck like he was trying to figure out what to say next to make me feel better about his boys and me this early in the morning.

"Yeah, you get them too on account-a me. That's how it works, Hank."

"How what works? Ry, I just don't know what you're talkin' about here …"

"Yeah," he took my hands from being perched at my waist into his own before continuing, choosing to kiss each finger softly as he continued, "about that. Can we talk about that later on today, like in the afternoon when we're alone? The guys are waitin' to see ya now." He looked at me from under his brow, with a look of concern that went straight to my heart.

"Can't you feel them none?"

I looked beyond us toward the ground, as if not looking at him would allow me to focus on the others. I was about to shake my head that I didn't feel a thing, when suddenly they were all there. Like soft caresses along my skin, I could feel each of them and knew instantly which touch belonged to which boy.

My eyes widened a bit. It was a bit much to take in. Riley's eyes widened with no small amount of fear in them, like he was scaring me or something, which in a real way, he was. Riley and Tanner was one thing. I wouldn't mind splitting my time between them. Tanner was a nice enough guy. Handsome as all get out, too. Prettier than a pumpkin, that boy is. Actually, as I thought about it, he was the only one of their bunch who never did give me a cause for worry or concern. And he and Maynard were as thick as thieves – as Mama liked to say – when they were young.

But Spike and the rest, I just didn't know.

"Hank, now, Hank." Riley put his hands on either side of my face again, getting me to look directly at him. The moment I did, everything, all my fears and doubts, melted away. As long as I saw him, I'd be okay.

"The boys ain't gonna *ever* hurt'cha or cause ya harm in no kinda way. Ya hear me?"

I nodded, only 'cause I couldn't think straight about nothing at the moment. Not when he looked at me like that.

"Ya trust me now, don'tcha?"

He looked up from under his brow at me again even though he was slightly taller than me; he had to lean forward a bit to do so. The thumbs from his hands gently caressed my cheeks and the side of my face so gentle-like. If he kept doing that I just knew I'd follow him to the ends of the Earth if he asked me.

"Good."

He pulled me forward and kissed my forehead. His lips sort of tickled as he spoke his next against it.

"You're about to become the most protected boy in this here county."

He pulled back again to get a proper look at me.

"And … the most loved."

I just didn't know what to say to that. It was all upside-down and backwards to how I was raised. Even though I knew I liked boys in that way, I always thought that it'd go unrequited — something I felt, but never in a million years could never act upon.

Yeah, well, that's certainly a thing of the past given Riley and I fuckin' out in the forest yesterday.

"We do, you know. All of us. You'll bind to the boys soon enough, I should think."

"What if …" I began, then thought better of it. I didn't really know what the "what if" I was gonna inquire about 'cause it hadn't truly formed yet. My mouth, as usual got ahead of my brain. He didn't seem to pay it no mind.

"What if what, Hank?" Then a look like he realized and put a name to what I couldn't even begin to sort out for myself.

"Ah, what if you don't want them like you want me?"

I shrugged. Yeah, 'cause it was as good as any.

He smirked and shrugged himself. "Never know'd it could be like that. Pack and all."

"What'd you mean by *pack*? I don't know what the hell is goin' on, Ry. Can'tcha give me a clue? Even a little?"

He sighed, and there was quite a bit behind that sigh, I could tell.

"It's sorta a package deal, Hank. You get me, you get the boys. It's just how it works, thassall."

"How *what* works?" I suddenly was ashamed for the whine that crept into my voice just then and at least had the mind to look ashamed I'd said it at all. I 'twasn't no sissy by any stretch but it sure as hell just sounded like I was. I knew shame was plain on my face just then. Riley smiled softly and ran his hands along my back, pulling me in a little tighter to him, our hips colliding enough that I could feel how much he wanted me right then.

"Tell ya what."

I lifted my chin at him so he knew he had my attention all clear like.

"Howzabout you just trust me on this. I take you to them and after you are around them a bit, you just signal to me that you want me to break it up and I will." His hands gripped the side of my face hard – forcing my eyes to snap to his. "I *promise*, Hank. Nothin' will give you a cause for worry if'n I'm around, got it?"

I gulped. I knew I wanted Riley. And I'd even accept Tanner, if that was the deal. But the rest of them made my stomach go a bit queasy on me. Not in a bad way, but just in a wary way. These were the boys who sort of made my day hell from time to time. Never outright teased me or nothin' … but still, they were a force to be reckoned with no matter where you fell in their food chain.

A pack, just like Ry had said.

He nodded once, smiled and then pulled back and held his hand out for me to take, which I sighed heavily and did. We slowly left the school and my things at the bleachers, and made our way into the forest.

To say that there was a great amount of trepidation or fear coursing through me woulda been the biggest understatement you could make.

But with the feel of Riley's hand holding mine, his numerous backward glances accompanied with a soft, and knowing smile, any resolve I had to put an end to this – which 'tweren't much I can tell you – would simply melt away. When he did that, I knew there'd be no turning back.

He was mine … (well, that's what he said)

It bore repeating often in my head 'cause I had to remind myself 'twas true.

We walked a piece by my reckoning before I picked up on their scents again: Toby, Mike, Maynard, Darby, Dylan, Tanner and of course, Spike.

As the boys came fully into view, I started to pull back again. Several years of taunting by them would've caused the same reaction in a stronger fella. Riley caught my suddenly not wanting to be near them and turned immediately to catch my eye.

I'm right here … you hear me inside, Hank?

His hands, big and rough, gripped the sides of my face as he stepped fully into view, blocking, the rest of them from my sight. Giving me a moment to get my bearings.

No one would dare harm you now. These boys are yours now. Don't reject them, Hank.

I shook my head slightly, not understanding the meaning of his words fully. He gripped my face a bit harder so I couldn't move and then his eyes went wide, or more like his pupils got large all of a sudden and I felt him like we was connected again, like yesterday when he was taking me so rough and hard. I felt him flush inside, soothing away everything inside of me, like I was his.

I was his …

NO ONE! Will. Harm. You. Now.

His voice reverberated inside every part of me like hollerin' down a well, making me quake just a bit at that overwhelming feeling of him moving about inside me.

He turned his head just a tad so I could see that he meant all of these boys now. I leaned my head slightly to look around him and he seemed to see this as a sign to release his hold on me. His right hand lingered a bit longer on the side of my face to bring my forehead to his lips.

He kissed it gently, speaking softly against it, "Just remember, *we* belong to you, Hank. These boys will do whatever you ask. They burn for you alone. Never forget that. Be kind to them. *You have the power to destroy them.*"

That caught my attention — I could *destroy* them? *What the blazes of hell did that mean?*

Like he heard what I was thinking he nodded just once and let me go, choosing to step aside and allow me to pass.

Trouble was, I didn't know if I wanted to.

I looked at them all, seven boys who, like me, were on the brink of becoming men. I'd always known they were well-bodied and strong boys, — 'cause their being athletes and all, I knew they worked hard at it. And it definitely showed. Four of them were in white T-shirts no doubt with rolled sleeves, just like that James Dean guy who was really big in the movies, complete with red cotton twill jackets what he wore. I saw *Rebel Without a Cause* in the movie theater in Beckley awhile back when it first came out. That movie made a big impression on me, for many reasons. These boys thought the same thing as well, 'cause I was looking at what coulda been four James Deans right in front of me. The other three were in tan pants and button down shirts with their letterman sweaters on.

They were awesome to behold.

Each boy was uniquely beautiful in his own way. They were alternatively pretty and handsome beyond compare. I could see why girls wanted to be with them, why the other boys wanted to run with them. They were beautiful, strong, men, in their prime.

They called to me, their scents rushing at me like arms longing to hold me close. I felt drawn to them. Each step I took toward them was easier than the last. Soon I was standing in the middle of the clearing and they were around me on nearly all sides. I turned my head slowly to look over my shoulder to where Riley stood with his arms crossed across his chest, a look of pride coloring him.

What did he have to be proud about? Certainly not me. I didn't know what was going on. I tried to put on a good face, that I was okay with this, when clearly inside I was anything but certain. None of this was making sense and yet some part of me knew what Riley said was true. I don't know how I can explain it; it was crazy, and made no kinda sense.

Yet, here we were.

They are mine, I thought.

As if they too could suddenly hear me they each nodded in turn and went to one knee — like those Errol Flynn movies, like Knights of the Round Table and all. Like they was pledging fealty to me. I walked forward a few steps, my slightly quivering hand slowly stretched out before me, reaching until it came into contact with Spike's face. The moment I touched him, he practically purred deep in his throat, inhuman in sound but deeply captivating, leaning the side of his face into my palm and gently rubbing it against him, like a pup would to get a good head scratch. I didn't know what to make of it.

Spike.

Raymond.

Raymond McGhee.

His purr went to a deep guttural growl in an instant. The other boys all sprang up and rounded on Spike. Spike's eyes narrowed – but his growl lost little of its threatening tone. I wanted to pull away from him, to go back to the comfort of Riley, but somehow I knew if I did, I'd be making a serious mistake. I didn't know how I knew this, but I did. Like something inside was guiding my hand, keeping me to some ancient course.

So instead I went with what suddenly sprang into my mind. My hand gripped his head hard by the short hairs on the back of his neck and he yelped like I'd stung him or something. His eyes went wide with shock. The other boys backed away slowly from me.

"You see, Hank. We *are* yours. *You* are in control. Always have been," Riley said as he slowly made his way to us, slipping easily between Dylan and Darby to come alongside me. He quirked his head to the side slightly and smirked a bit. My eyes moved slowly between them both, unsure of how to handle this, but wanting Riley to continue. "You just need to take up the reins, is all."

He slowly approached me.

"Though Spike here, always seems to give us a bit of grief."

Riley slipped an arm around my waist and placed his chin on my shoulder so he could speak directly into my ear.

"But he'll heel, if you tell him to." He glanced at Spike before returning to me, "He doesn't have a choice."

I could feel Riley turn to look at Spike directly.

"Do ya, Spike?"

Spike only whimpered as he nodded briefly his agreement. I let my hand slip from him. He looked at me sheepishly as he stood up and moved in with the rest of the boys who had gathered around me. Their scents were stronger. I could smell each of them, their distinct musk filled my senses. I knew I was learning each of them, like my body and mind was memorizing them, an imprint, an impression on me what I knew would never be erased. When at last I found my voice, it surprised even me what came out of it. I turned slowly around, taking each of them in turn, their eyes meeting mine, connecting with me.

"I don't know what all of this means. I feel like I am fumbling around in the dark with y'all. I mean, yesterday I was one of your chew toys – something to be tossed around and forgotten. Now, well, I don't know what this is. I mean, once Riley and me fu— ..."

I stopped, panic no doubt all over my face that it nearly all came out – my gaze moved quickly to his, fearful that he'd be angry that I'd put word to what we done.

Riley only chuckled softly, his eyes brilliant with whatever remembrances from our brief union yesterday. I felt myself blush deeply under that gaze.

"They know about that, Hank. It's part of it all."

I spun around on him so quickly the boys sort of jumped back a pace or two, surprised as I was about it all.

"What the fuck is that supposed to mean, Ry? How could they?" I looked around at them all, and there was a recognition I couldn't mistake. They *did* know – from the looks of it, nearly as intimately as Riley and I did.

This was beyond anything I coulda feared. In an instant I turned and burst through them and took off at a run. As I passed Riley I gave him a look of absolute terror. I know I did little to avoid it.

"I can't do this ... I can't do any of this ..." I murmured to him as I passed.

I pushed my way through the brush and trees as quickly as I could. I could hear them calling after me, giving chase, which only made me press even harder to get away.

"Hank! No ... WAIT! You don't understand ..." I could hear the fear and the anguish in Riley's voice. It tugged upon my chest with such intensity that it was like a forty pound weight on it bringing my run to a complete stop. I dropped to my knees gripping my chest. Hands were on me rolling me over onto my back.

"No, no, no, no! HANK! C'mon, Hank ... listen to me!" Riley was running his hands along my face bringing my head to his lap as gentle as can be. "Baby, you need to listen to me. Breathe, just breathe through it. You're connected to all of us. If one of us *feels* something intensely you'll feel it tenfold."

Inwardly, the pain intensified. I tried to push at it, like I could paw at it, scratching it out. I began to pant with the exertion.

"Hank!" Riley barked at me.

My eyes snapped to his words, though none of my harsh breathing subsided. I was really starting to panic, trembling uncontrollably. I just wanted it all to stop.

Riley's eyes were wide with fear. He was trying really hard to talk me down, to make me see a way to calm myself. I could feel all of them doing it but it was like they were outside a great wall and couldn't get past it. I was alone, and falling into this well of pain that wouldn't stop.

"HANK! HANK! Listen to me! Find me!"

His hands were on either side of my face, the trembling was overtaking any thought I …

couldn't …

st-st-st-st-op …

…

Warmth. Like a match to tinder — it caught and poured through me like a flood of lava like I learned about them volcanoes in Hawaii. It surrounded me … no, not it, *him*.

Riley.

As his lips caressed mine, his tongue dove into my mouth, he poured everything he felt about me inside. He coursed through me, soothing, calming the tremors wherever they occurred. I wanted to pull that warmth around me like a blanket.

So I did.

Inwardly, I fell into Riley.

Into the black.

And the oddest thing happened as I let go and fell, I heard the growls and low rumble of wolves. It should've frightened me. Instead, somehow I found it strangely comforting.

Falling …

Darkness …

"Well, he's got to find out before too long. The 31st ain't all that long off!" I heard Spike holler at the boys.

Why couldn't he just quiet down? I felt so drained. So damned tired, like I could just roll over and sleep until next spring.

As my mind became clearer I realized that they were talking about me; and they were talking openly about it.

"He's gonna find out by then anyway. He's gonna lose his shit over it if'n we don't figure out how to get him to understand what he is!" Spike griped.

"And just what is that, Spike? Do you know? 'Cause, way I see it none of us know what he is to us. We asked around, none of the others know what we got here. They never heard of an *Omega* who has the pull that *he* has on all of us," Darby barked out, not bothering to hide the snarl to his voice.

I could hear him moving about as he ranted at Spike and the others. I kept my eyes closed as I listened to them argue. I figured if I kept quiet and still then I might just discover what was going on. I did what I could to relax as much as I could and pay attention.

"And what the fuck was that, that happened to him anyhow?" Mike chimed in. "Why'd he freak out like that, Riley? I thought you said he'd be stronger than all of us. That he was what would make us the strongest pack in this here state and I gotta admit, yeah, we can all feel him. Fuck, in that way he's so beyond anything I've ever felt. So yeah, I get that. But jess look at him now. He's a gaummed up mess!"

It was quiet as they all considered Mike's words. I heard some grunts of agreement from the others. Could they all feel what I was feeling?

"BUT!" I could hear him move toward me, the rocks and dirt crunching under his feet as he drew nearer. "Why'd he fall apart like that until you went and kissed him, Riley? Answer me that."

I could hear him panting. He was scared; all of them were to a degree. Well, except Riley and Tanner for some reason I couldn't begin to guess. They were all upset and it took me a great deal of my own resolve to keep that feeling pressed down, push it all away. It was a struggle to do that and just make it seem like I was still asleep.

"Later, Mike," Riley mumbled.

"Later? Why? I asked a question and I think we'd all like to hear the answer."

"Yeah? Well while all you busy Bettys have been yappin' like your Mas over the fence at each other, you all ain't took notice that our boy Hank has been awake for the past few minutes listenin' to us."

I could feel them all as they took his words in and their emotions rolled away with that like some massive change in a river current. That's what they felt like, water, coursing around me. Their emotions about me was strong. I realized they were all looking at me now. So I began to pick myself up. I slowly sat up, careful not to catch their eyes. I didn't think I could take their hard looks or harsh words about me.

I thought they'd all be feeling like I was weak and pitiful, that I'd ruined everything. I slowly lifted my head, expecting to see the worst reflected back to me. But I didn't see that at all. What I saw was each of them just as concerned about me as they could be.

Riley stood there, a look of such love on his face I didn't know quite what to make of it. Part of me wanted to pick up where I'd left off — run, take flight. But I knew they'd come after me.

Bound to me … that's what they'd said.

It started to make some kinda sense, even if I didn't fully understand it all. I could feel them all anchored to my heart. Like invisible threaded lines that glowed so bright in my mind that I almost thought you could see them.

Bringing my knees up to me, I huddled in, wrapping my arms around myself across my chest, feeling suddenly colder than before even though the sun was higher in the sky.

"How long was I, ya know, out?" I asked.

"Bout ten minutes …" Riley said softly as he walked toward me, "give or take …" he winked which made me smile the tiniest bit. This seemed to please them all. The mood lightened considerably like they could feel what I was feeling or something.

"Look, uh, I don't know what this is all about. I don't know how to act around y'all. Everything is just so … *queer*, off, not right." I spared a look at them all.

My eyes quickly darted from one to the other. In each case they looked right back at me but not with disgust as I thought, but with nothing but pure affection. And I knew then that I was wrong in what I said. For some reason I couldn't put together it was queer, because it was decidedly different. It was off, but because I didn't know how to act or take what they were giving to me.

But it was this last part where I'd gone completely off the rails, 'cause it was anything *but* being *not* right. It was exactly the opposite: it was *very* right. They slowly moved toward me and I started to get up and take a step or two back cause I didn't know what they was doing. Then my backside ran right into Riley (*when'd he move to get on the other side of me?*)

who didn't budge or give me any way to take my leave of them. Instead, he held me firmly in place with his hands holding onto my hips and his grip was strong, powerfully so.

His message was clear: I wasn't going anywhere. It was time I faced my boys and what it meant. I was really gonna do this. Only problem was, I didn't quite know what *this* was. I didn't have to wait long to find out.

The boys moved in really close, each of them, in turn, nuzzling into my neck, sniffing of me deeply, before their lips met my own. With a few of them plundering my mouth as much as Riley had. I should've been alarmed. I shoulda pushed each of them away. I only wanted Riley, didn't I?

This was definitely *queer*.

Only, if I was being truly honest, it wasn't. Not at all …

With each boy nuzzling in, sharing their mouths, their tongues with my own — with some running their hands along my chest or face – I could feel my body wanting to lay claim each of them. I responded to each of them. Spike was the last one to step up. He looked over my shoulder pointedly at Riley. I glanced over my shoulder to see how Riley was reacting and saw that he not only lifted his hands from my hips, but he held them up in a slight surrender.

Convinced that I was standing there on my own, Spike reached up slowly, his hands pausing as my head leaned back as if I thought he was going to strike me for being so rough with him earlier.

"Hank …" he said softly, his eyes were practically pleading with me. "I could never hurt you. Not ever. You understand me? I know you think we've all been pickin' on ya. I know that you thought we'd all been givin' ya shit, but you gotta understand that we'd only been doin' it 'cause we had to see what you was made of, thassall. But Hank, you gotta believe me."

He moved his hands again from where they had been suspended in the air before me – so anxious to touch me but not daring to do so for fear that I'd do something about it – to slowly take my face in them. He ran a gentle thumb across my right cheek.

"Riley is right. *We are yours.* All of us, Hank. I know they all say I'm the smart ass, the wild card. But, you listen here … *are ya listenin' to me, Hank?* 'Cause I want you to be clear about this, 'K?"

I slowly nodded.

"*No one*, and I mean this as sure as I am livin' and breathin' here, *no one* is gonna touch you without the whole lot of us boys takin' 'em down: I give my life to you. I ain't mincin' words here or tryin' to be all fancy like. There's a real reason why we feel the way we do, why this is happenin' to all of us. And ya gotta believe me, Hank. It's not the usual way. 'Cause we'd all be lyin' if we said otherwise. There are rules, there's a way we all gonna be together now, only, well, only you are sort of breakin' all of them. Ain't anyone we've talked to that can say anything like you has ever happened."

"Any of what?" I hated that gall durn whine in my voice again, but I was sort of desperate here.

Spike sighed, and 'twasn't a simple sigh neither. That sigh had quite a bit behind it, it seemed. He needed me in a way I couldn't understand or begin to describe; it just was. Inside something clicked into place about all of them. Some part of me understood this.

Tumblers in a lock, that's the only way to describe it.

I returned the same to Spike by placing my hands on either side of his face and bringing his mouth to my own, using his tongue to drink from me. He nearly buckled from that kiss. Whatever I'd done to him with that kiss he wasn't prepared for. Fearing for his well-being I released him and he staggered back a step or two, panting and shaking his head out as if I'd just clopped him one. Then he smiled, a dark and wickedly sly smile, "Whooo-doggie boys! That's one helluva Omega. Look at him – he ain't even winded by it and I'm shakin' like a leaf in the wind!" He panted some before he lunged for me again.

"I need me some more of that!"

That grin turned lustful within seconds and he came at me and pulled me from Riley entirely and wrapped his arms around me tightly and attacked my mouth with such vigor that I literally felt a pull from him, like his lapping tongue in my mouth was feeding him in ways I couldn't begin to guess. The pull was strong, but I found I had only more to give him no matter how much he took in that kiss.

Then I really began to feel it. Intense bursts of color going off in my head and heart. The boys were deeply aroused. I could smell them. If I didn't put a stop to it something I didn't think we were prepared for was gonna happen. I pushed him away a bit and he fought me, trying to paw at my body to where the other guys had to move in and separate us. The shouts for Spike to back off quickly became growls and snarls and then the dust began to fly until Riley cut through them all with a snarl so fierce that it made *me* jump. He quickly pulled me to him and Tanner moved in to keep me tucked between them as they stared down the other boys.

I couldn't help myself and my eyes darted to their crotches of their pants, mostly 'cause I needed to confirm that what I smelled was what I thought it was.

It was.

Each boy was fully aroused and I could tell they wanted to do me as much as Riley had the day before.

We belong to you now. They all intoned in my head as one.

I started to get what they was trying to say to me all along. I was just too danged dense to put it together before.

I had now.

I could tell with that realization that they all knew I knew what they wanted. And I also knew that at some point it'd probably come to pass. Looks like I didn't have me just one boyfriend now; I had eight. I nearly passed out at that thought alone.

"Now you boys listen up," Riley practically growled at them. "He's figured out just how far this goes but he ain't ready. I know it and you'n know it. Give the boy some space. It's in our blood. All of us. He's just beginnin' to feel what we all have had two years to sort out. We're bound about as much as we can be until he turns. It's pretty unbreakable now but you all know our world. The deed ain't sealed until we truly bind to him."

There was a moment so taut it was like a bow being pulled back to the point of breaking, only I could tell that the boys did respect Riley as their leader. Didn't do much about the way they was all hard up to have a go with me, but I could see that whatever Riley was doing was bringing them down a notch or two at a time.

"So here's what's gonna happen. We all got school today. Hank *needs* a normal day. You got that?"

He looked around at each of them, when there wasn't much of a response, he snarled again and the boys took a moment to check each other, then they nodded and looked down at the ground.

"So you keep those snakes in your drawers and give Hank some breathin' room. Just think how it'd be if'n you was the one who was in the center of everythin' … right?"

They shrugged a bit here and there but not very convincing. That wasn't good enough for Riley, it seemed.

"God dammit, I said, *right?*"

They all answered yes as a group and at least had the good intention of looking like scolded pups about it, for which I was truly thankful, even if my own body was aching for each of them just now. I tried like hell to push it back into the black.

"Now, you all need to use your influence to keep the rest of the school from takin' too much notice of how we're all reactin' to Hank. And I *know* you need to spend time with him. I get it."

"Sure ya do, you already are bound to him. We can smell it on ya. 'Tain't fair, is all I'm sayin' …" Spike bit out.

I knew what they were talking about and on some level I was aroused by the thought too. What did that make me, some sort of *whore* for them?

Wrong dang move, dammit.

They all snapped their heads up the moment I thought the word *whore* and growled fiercely. Riley and Tanner included. Riley took a deep breath and calmed himself, holding his hands out to the other boys, to ward them off, before he turned to face me.

"Hank, you just gotta be careful thinkin' them thoughts. We can *hear* you." He touched the side of his own head and then to his heart.

"We're bound to you. I know you can feel it. The boys aren't as strong as you and me are but that'll come in time. But you can't think things like what you thought there. It's in our nature to defend what's ours. And you are the most sacred thing to us. Thinkin' you was some kinda …" he clenched his eyes to the word, he couldn't say it out loud, which made me fall in love with him again, "well, you know what I mean. It'll just get the boys, *and me*, riled up. That's not a good thing if'n that ain't what you want. Okay? I know, well, uh, we know, that all of this is so confusing."

He turned back to the boys but kept glancing back my way to ensure that I was following along just so I know'd I was included in what he was saying. He eyed each of them, making it clear that his word was law.

"Anyway, we each spend some part of our day with Hank in the same class. You are to sit next to him no matter where he sits. You are to keep him close at all times. You don't let him walk somewhere alone from now on. We protect what's ours. Do your duty, boys. Keep him safe. Y'all know why. If we lose him, well, then … *we're all lost.*"

The boys had collected themselves from their wilder selves a few minutes ago and started to behave as I'd always known them. It didn't mean that my day was gonna be any more normal than before, 'cause I wasn't kidding myself that it was.

Things were definitely going to be different and on a scale I could scarce imagine.

I stupidly thought I had me my first boyfriend.

Now it looks like I have eight.

Well, Mama is just gonna shit …

Needless to say, school was an exercise in the absurd. Everywhere I'd go, I was surrounded by, at the very least, three of the pack. Truth be told, I didn't have a class where Spike was in it but dang it all if he didn't tag along for every class I had that day. Seems my kiss with him had made him loopy for me. He whispered that he *wasn't lettin' me outta his sight fer nuttin'.*

And he 'twasn't the only one, neither.

Lunch was a mess of whispers and covert finger-pointing that I just know'd was gonna get back to Mama and Cory, mostly 'cause I didn't have many friends and now it looked like I had me one of them big followings like them movie stars did. Only I didn't do nothing to have a cause to have one. Not the way I saw it, that is.

But I need never pay it any mind 'cause 'twasn't like I had a choice in the matter. These boys stuck to me like the sap off a pine tree, equal parts sticky and bittersweet.

There was one big benefit to my whole new life at Cavanagh: the girls that the boys had played with before 'tweren't even catching their eyes now. I decided I'd let myself take that in for a spell, but even I know'd it was too much to ask that it'd last much longer before someone would say something what couldn't be took back.

After the bell sounded on my PE period, which was the last of the day, I made my way with the other boys back to the locker room to shower and change.

Before today, this was the fastest part of any of my days at Cavanagh. I usually got back to the locker room, stripped and was at the shower for the fastest danged scrub up you ever did see. You'd thought my backside was on fire with the way I moved about washing and scrubbing fast and furious just so I could get my naked butt back into my school clothes and out for the trip back home.

'Cept of course, like the rest of my day today, this time it was gonna be different.

When I got to my locker not only were Darby and Dylan there to meet me, even though their lockers were a couple of aisles over from my own, but so were the other guys too. Rising up like a forest of massive trees as I rounded the corner, I had me eight of the football team standing around my locker like it was the most normal thing to do – intimidation just pouring from them all – it was embarrassing to say the least. I was gonna have some words with them all after school let out.

"I can shower myself, ya know. Been doin' it just fine for years," I mumbled as I wove my way through them and sat on the bench, pissed as a cornered polecat.

The guys smirked with a few of them shaking their heads like what I'd just said was the craziest thing that coulda *ever* come outta my mouth.

Yeah, I was the crazy one here.

I sat there, facing my locker with my elbows on my knees and my head in my hands, knowing that this was definitely gonna make the rounds at school. Those tongues would be a-wagging like two old biddies at a quilting bee.

Riley sat down next to me but facing the other direction.

"Hank …" he said softly as he turned and ran a hand down my back, trying to soothe away my nervous feelings about all of this. I shrugged it off hard and he pulled back like I stung him or something; I didn't fucking care at this point. I was so angry and embarrassed I just know'd tears were gonna fall at any minute which only served to add salt to injury as Cory'd like to say.

Even though I just know'd that they could all feel me collapsing inside, they gave me my space. They let me have my moment to just work through it. Sad part was, I knew 'twasn't gonna change. This was how it was gonna be now. My boys were closing up around me like something was gonna happen.

And that thought alone had me concerned. *What could be so danged threatening?*

Trouble was, what they was doing was so danged public. That's what had me worried. Someone was gonna say something sooner or later; it was bound to happen. Even I wasn't so starry-eyed not to see that coming a mile off.

I could hear the guys from my gym period clear out, their conversations more hushed than usual. They had stripped, showered and changed and were all nearly gone while I sat here surrounded by pillars of meat and bone that wouldn't let me move so much as a muscle to get cleaned up myself. They didn't say anything; they didn't have'ta. I could feel it pouring off of them. I am sure that the football team all-stars hanging around my locker throwing their manliness around the room like they was taking a piss to claim me was a sight to behold. 'Cause that's what it felt like, like they was marking their territory – *me*.

I just didn't want to think about it. Riley sighed and ran his hand through his hair. I knew I was upsetting him.

Good …

If they could truly feel what I was thinking then I wouldn't have to explain what I was thinking, 'cause they'd know it for theyselves.

Suddenly, I heard someone walk up behind us and I finally pulled my head out of my hands and turned around with the rest of them.

"You're good …" Coach Thompson said with a nod, tossing the keys to Riley who caught them and then the coach left the locker room – hearing the door click closed behind him.

"'Kay boys, you heard the man, shower time," was all Riley said, as if that were the most normal thing that could've been said at this time.

"Wait a goll durn minute!" I called out, stopping each of them in turn from yanking themselves outta their clothes. I slowly stood up. "Just what the *fuck* do you think is going to go down here?"

I couldn't catch my breath. I could feel them all around me – I could smell them: aroused.

"I ain't that kinda boy!" I bellowed at them.

Riley snarled deeply, his voice loomed over the room. Even I shrank from him, pulling myself up against the row of lockers though not a step further on account of being surrounded by half-naked boyfriends.

My life had officially done gone cattywampus.

Riley turned on me and pressed his finger into my chest pushing me right up against the locker.

"Look, I know we ain't all been straight wit ya. I git it. But I swear as God is my witness that if you ever suggest that what you are ain't pure or that we'd think so lowly of ya that you can just say or insinuate that you are somethin' that we would ever *think* of defilin', then you just better think ag'in. Ya git me?"

I just watched him wide-eyed. He scared me something fierce. For the first time I saw why these boys followed Riley with such dedication. He was awesome scary when he raged like this. I swear he almost looked like an animal. I'd swear on a stack o' Bibles his eyes practically glowed a brilliant amber. For the first time ever I almost painted the insides of my shorts just from the look he was giving me.

He caught himself, pulling up short before he actually got too close. He shook for a second before he got himself under control.

"Now," he was panting, his breaths coming at me in heated bursts, "we gotta do what we gotta do. I know you don't know what's goin' on and believe me Hank, I'd like nuttin' more than to tell ya. I would. But, well," he ran a hand through his hair to calm himself further, "me and the boys reckon that you couldn't handle it if we was to lay it all out fer ya. It'd be too much. You'd *really* paint the inside of yer shorts if you knew. So, please, Hank. Trust me on this and just go along with what we'd be doin' here. 'Cause in a few days it'll all become clearer. I *promise* you."

He came up to me slowly, his hands held up in front of me in surrender. I know I shook a tiny bit as he did so, my eyes moving from each of the boys who were watching what was going on with a look of concern in how I was reacting to all of this. My eyes came back to Riley as he slipped his hand around my neck and brought my forehead against his.

"I'll say it ag'in 'cause it bears repeatin', I guess," he whispered.

His gaze into my eyes was powerfully strong; I couldn't look away if I tried.

"You is the greatest, most prodigious thing that coulda ever happened to us. We don't know why it is," he chuckled softly and I could feel the boys join in that feeling. "But it just is. We been told that what's happenin' here, with you, is really shakin' things up and that it's definitely diff'rent. So we're sorta workin' our way through it too. And look, I know you're scared about all of this – the not knowin' and all. But you gotta know we's tryin' real hard to make it as easy as we can fer ya. And I *swear* to ya, it will make sense in a few days. Can you just hang in there 'til then? Can you do that for us, Hank? Fer *me*?"

He kissed me, slow and tender-like and my fear just melted. Intense feelings from the boys washed over us as he held me to him.

I stood there, slightly dazed, as he pulled back, my gaze slowly moving to the others, frightened a little at what I might see.

"'S'all right boys, I think Hank's gonna be just fine," Riley said to them without breaking his gaze upon me. I could still feel his breaths against my neck. I wanted him something fierce at that moment, I can tell you what.

"Go on now, get the shower ready."

The boys slowly resumed getting undressed, whispering quietly to each other and I noticed that they were all giving glances what said far more than their words did and they just seemed to know what the other was thinking.

A sensation along my stomach brought my attention to Riley as he nuzzled into my neck and began to pull my shirt up and over my head. He continued to clear away the rest of my gym clothes, taking care with my shoes and socks, running his thumbs along the tops of my feet like they was the most interesting things he ever did see, a gentle thumb along each of my toes. All the while he kept humming that song by the Platters that was big last year on the radio. I couldn't remember the name until he got to a point in the song where it came to me: *Only You.* That was certainly telling. Seems Riley had quite the voice. It was warm like a blanket on a cold winter morning, soothing and gentle but definitely a man's voice. I rather liked him singing to me, crooning to me like he was doing.

When Riley'd removed my shoes he sat on the bench but now that he'd done that it was the moment what made my breath catch in my throat. I didn't expect what he was gonna do next. Instead of removing my jock he leaned in and nuzzled against my privates, inhaling deeply, a low guttural roll to his throat. His eyes was closed as he took me in. He was practically purring from it all, a sweet warm purr to his throat. He slowly shook his head back and forth a bit, forcing my legs further apart so he could really breathe me in. He seemed to like it a great deal. My musk and sweat was doing something for him. I could smell it on him too. He was deeply aroused. A gentle sweep of his tongue, now and again, made me bite my lower lip to stifle the small whimper what struggled to break free.

I didn't know how to react. I mean, we'd fucked already. Riley was my lover. So I would never deny him access to my body. He's as much as said we was together, didn't he? That was obvious. I ran a hand through his hair as he began to lick and nuzzle me deeply. I was growing hard from it all. That was bad. It had to be, didn't it?

Riley stopped what he was doing to me and slowly stood up, making sure that as he did so he brought his body closer to my own. Being I was pressed up against the lockers I didn't have much in the way of escape – except when Riley was this close, I didn't wanna move no how.

His eyes were dark, like he'd take me right there if I let him. Thing was, I would, in front of the guys and everything. If it was Riley, he could do what he wanted when he wanted. He had to know that. He had to see that in my eyes.

What did that say about me?

Riley pressed his lips to mine, the smell of me on his face. For reasons I couldn't quite explain to myself it only served to make me even harder.

He pressed against me, grinding his hips into my own as the kiss got heavier. His hands slipped down my body, gripped the jockstrap and with one powerful force he ripped it from me and flung it across the room.

Ma was gonna be pissed about that. It was still a good jock strap.

He released me, panting heavily and he slowly shucked out of his clothes. His eyes never strayed from mine unless the deed called for it, which thankfully wasn't but twice. Each time though, I thought my heart was gonna fall right out the bottom of my feet.

As he removed his shoes and socks I looked around and noticed that all of the boys had cleared away. Where'd they all go?

Showers, I supposed.

Riley stood up just as naked to the world as I was, his cock jutting out just as proud and strong as my own. He just smirked and then before I could do or say anything to the contrary, he scooped me up and kissed me gently, rubbing my nose against his, his eyes drinking me in as he walked us to where I could hear the showers running and realized that this was where the boys had collected themselves.

We was gonna shower together now? And the Coach knew about this? What did that mean? Riley looked into my eyes again and just shook his head slightly.

"In a few days … okay? All of it will be clearer. But the boys need this; they need you. They's hurting something fierce and I can't make it right. They know it's coming from you. It's gotta be you what fixes 'em up right. You'll see. Just trust me, okay?"

I knew that it shouldn't be easy for him to carry me like he was. I mean I knew he was a big man now, but I wasn't no wilting flower neither. Yet he didn't seem like he was straining much at all. There was a part of me that sort of enjoyed being with him like that. Not that I'd ever admit that out loud or nothing … just letting myself take it in for what it was.

As we came around the corner to the shower area he slowly set me down as navigating the wet surface was probably going to be a bit more difficult with me taking so much of him as we passed through the doorway.

I came around the door jamb and there they were: seven boys on the brink of being some of the finest specimen of men what I ever did see. I didn't expect Hollywood woulda been able to come up with a collection of young men as I had before me, caught in the muted shards of shadow and light from the clerestory windows along the top of the room, the water splashing against their skin. Each of those boys was singularly beautiful – my breath hitched – I suddenly found I couldn't get air easily into my lungs. I wanted to run, knowing full well that I couldn't do such a thing. These boys would definitely give chase and I didn't want to be the one to cause these boys the embarrassment of chasing me across the football field without a stitch on – because they wouldn't spare a moment to get dressed – they'd be out that door chasing me like their lives depended upon it. Ry's words still slithered across my mind.

"Just remember, we belong to you, Hank. These boys will do whatever you ask. They burn for you alone. Never forget that. Be kind to them. You have the power to destroy them."

No doubt feeling the brunt of my resistance, Ry pressed behind me, the prodding of his prodigious member cleaving its way between the cleft of my ass. I knew what he wanted, only 'cause deep down it was what I wanted as well. I just didn't plan having an audience the next time I had Ry take me as thoroughly as he had yesterday.

His arms slithered around my waist with his hands moving up along my chest to slightly tweak upon my nipples, making my cock bounce as if they had a direct line to it. I tried like hell to suppress a yelp of satisfaction. Ry only chuckled against my ear as he pulled the lobe into his mouth, making me tremble in his arms.

"These boys are yours, Hank. Never forget, you are in control here."

I nodded slowly.

"So, uh, whassupposed to hap-p-pen now?" I couldn't keep the shake out of my voice no matter how hard I tried.

He turned me slightly so he could look me in the eye, "Why? What do you *think* is supposed to happen now?"

I was about to open my mouth when the most salacious grin mellowed along his lips.

"They're gonna wash you, of course. They need to be near you, touch you, taste you. The bindin' won't be for a few days now but, for now, as much contact with you the better it would be for all of them. The calmer they'll be. And, uh," he looked at each of them, "they'll do you a whole hill-a good too. Look at them, Hank. *Really* look at them."

I turned slightly. They were all still there lookin' at me, lathering themselves up but in that way that allowed the soap to move along the rise and fall of each muscle of their hard bodies.

Looking at them now, the scent of soap and man filling every corner of the shower area, I felt them collectively pull me from Ry, like their bodies were calling me and I was helpless to stop it if I wanted to. And dang it all if I didn't realize that I really didn't want it to be like that. Plain and simple: I wanted them. I wanted them as much as they were wanting me.

I took my time to move slowly toward the middle of the shower area. As I reached it the boys moved from the shower heads that lined the outer wall and as if like some carefully staged dance, they moved to meet me. Slowly stalking me. I glanced over my shoulder to see if Riley stayed put, and there he was, just leaning up against the wall and gently, but purposefully, stroking the length of his considerable shaft, a small stream of pre-cum dripping like honey from a spout. Involuntarily, I licked my lips. I wanted nothing more than to lave my tongue on his cock. I knew the taste of him would satisfy what I could now feel building deep inside my belly. And for some reason I couldn't quite get, I realized that my thinking they *were* a pack seemed so right. I could feel it in that room. Like gnats on a hot summer day, the air was thick with it. They were connected.

No Hank, we' re connected. We need you in ways we can't even put to words. To us, you are life itself. I know that's a lot to take in. But you'll see. Once we're bound – once we are one – we'll be unstoppable. And you're the key to all of this. The boys know it. I know it, too.

I don't know why, but the more Ry talked in my head, the more I kinda liked it. It made me feel less alone in the world somehow.

My eyes moved slowly around, taking a moment to look each approaching boy in the eye, making dang sure that they see me as much as I was seeing them. They were too – and dang it all if those boys scents didn't overwhelm me. Mingled with the soap that covered their hard bodies was the arousal of their sex. And there was no mistaking it; they were directing it solely at me.

Tanner reached me first, for which I was glad, for I'd sorta been with him already – well kinda. As if he heard my thoughts loud and clear between Riley and me, he leaned forward so his forehead could touch against mine, and he said ever so softly, "You ain't ever gonna have a lonely day in your life, Hank O'Malley. We's apart of you now, ya hear?"

He pulled me to him in a cascade of water from the shower behind me and kissed me deeply and I melted. I melted in ways I didn't think was possible with another man. His strong arms and large frame almost eclipsed my own. He began to moan a little, a gentle rumble in his throat and chest. Then I felt something other than water splashing against my hip and I realized he just erupted on me. His cock was throbbing and bouncing against my hip and the rich scent of him nearly knocked me over. Every smell and sense seemed overwhelming.

Darby, who was next to us ran his fingers along my hip and took some of Tanner's spent fluids and slipped it into his mouth before he gently turned my face to his. Before I could think of what was gonna happen next, we kissed too. The taste of Tanner and Darby was even greater than before. The two of them were doing things to my body and mind that made me lose all rational thought.

Binding ... bound. Those words kept repeating.

Each boy in turn had their moment with me, tasting, releasing themselves all over me, like I was bathing in them all. Each one was different; each one I could recall every subtle and slight change between them, their flavor, their scent, the very essence of who they were as men. They were in my system now. I could suddenly feel every little bit of them inside of me, a solid line connecting me to them. Each of them with that final boy once again being Spike.

It was life altering, that was – nothing short of it.

Then Tanner took me from Spike who still didn't seem to know when his turn was over with me. I had to remember that about him. Spike was every bit the firebrand his dark auburn hair alluded to. Tanner growled deeply; that sound only served to make me harder. He pulled me so my back was to his front and I saw what he was directing me toward: Riley.

Ry stood there, hidden in the shadows of the glow of the afternoon light pouring from those highly placed windows above, yet I could still see him as plain as day, like the darkness couldn't hide nothing from me no more.

He smirked, a wicked kind of smile. I had one for him in return. The taste of the boys still fresh upon my tongue, filling my nostrils, flooding my senses. The other boys stood nearby, leaning into each other, playing with themselves and sharing kisses and nuzzling each other. If I was just seeing this for the first time, I swore I'd've been gobsmacked for days after. Only now, they were a part of me, inside me and all. What they were doing to one another just seemed right, just seemed like we were all one. I could feel each of them too. Mike along my left arm, Darby and Toby coursing through my legs. I knew they were in my blood now. I could feel them eke into every part of me, along with Riley, who was still the most dominant sensation. They followed him, but it was a team.

A pack.

Pack …

That word kept circling in my head. I know I thought it the first time on account of because of our team mascot, the wolves. But now, it seemed to have a new meaning.

As Riley started to move toward me I saw that he hadn't yet relieved himself. He was hard, incredibly so, and so fucking beautiful in that way boys can be all wet and slicked up like that. I wanted him. I wanted him something fierce.

He moved into take me – his one arm slinking around my waist and the other came up around my neck, holding me still – letting me know he was in control now.

He shook his head the tiniest bit. *Oh yeah, I was always in control.*

He smirked again and nodded that I had it right.

He leaned forward, his lips barely touching my own; his words so soft that even above the rushing water of the showers, I could still hear him as if he were talking right into my ear.

"I need to taste you, lover, okay?"

It took me a second or two before I realized the fullness of what he was saying to me. He smiled, then kissed me, that now familiar deep guttural purr to that kiss that went straight to my dick, making it so hard it ached for release. He pressed his body up against mine backing me into Tanner even more. I was like a big sandwich between them. Tanner nuzzled into my right ear, purring a bit himself and I felt him tease my backside with his rather large cock. It was the one thing we all seemed to share equally; It seemed we were all packing quite a bit downstairs. Or maybe I just didn't realize how most boys were. While I liked them and all, I did everything I could *not to look* before. Now I couldn't get enough of looking at them, each set of cock and balls just as beautiful as the next.

And it seemed they was mine, now.

Riley pulled back the tiniest bit, speaking into my mouth in that way that made me want to kiss him again.

"Tanner's my beta, Hank. You know what that means?"

I didn't really but I just nodded once. Riley chuckled softly; no fooling him, I guess.

"It means that he's my second, the guy who backs me up no matter what. So he's the next to be with you. He needs you, Hank. Can't you feel how much?"

I did feel it. His rigid cock was cleaving its way between my ass cheeks and gently, but forcefully prodding at me. I knew now what Ry was saying to me.

"Now, Tanner's a bit rough when he fucks. He's a big guy – in ev'ry way. I know. We've been fucking off and on for a while now. But I know you got it in you to deal with it. Tanner will test ya though."

Riley's eyes flashed in the light. I swear it musta been just how the soft sunlight bounced off the water in the room. It had to be.

"Just not today, Tanner. 'K? You be lovin' now, ya hear?"

Before I could say anything Tanner began to press forward, breeching me and cleaving me in two. Instead of a cry of pain like I expected, I felt a grumble take root in my throat and bubble its way up and out. The boys around us began to purr loudly too, each of them stroking themselves, quickly matching the rhythm that Tanner was taking me over and over. Tanner slipped his large arms up under my pits and gripped my shoulders, keeping me firmly in place as he continued to take me in long thrusts bringing me to the tips of my toes without relenting in his fucking. I felt myself gradually open to him, each driving thrust making me quake inside. I threw my head back against his chest and my eyes rolled back. I lost all visual sensation at that point.

Then my cock was surrounded by wet warmth: Riley, had to be. I forced my eyes to open and looked down at him on his knees before me, sucking at me like I was gonna feed him something he desperately needed.

Tanner was unrelenting – he was damn near brutal with each successive thrust into me, he nipped at my neck and ear, his tongue finding its way to my ear canal and lapping at it as he drove into me. I felt myself clench hard upon him and he moaned deeply and his body shuddered. Another thrust and he erupted deep inside. I felt him cumming hard and fast. I couldn't hold out. I tried to nudge Riley away from me – thinking for some reason he'd be upset if I didn't warn him. But Ry just batted my hand away and began to suck me with such force that I came hard and fast with the last thrusts of Tanner, as if my cumming was an extension of his own.

Riley slowly stood. His body shook with what looked like sheer pleasure. Each of the boys moved toward him and he kissed them each – they became heated again and relieved themselves on Riley as they tasted me from his mouth.

When it seemed like all were satisfied, Tanner nuzzled me and I felt such a rush of love from him filling every square inch of me that I was simply amazed that it could be like this between boys.

I didn't know what sex was like with girls. Not that there weren't girls who'd hinted at it with me, but I always seemed to be at a loss of what to do. Since Daddy 'twasn't around no more, I didn't have any way of asking how it was all done between men and women. It just seemed like an awful lot of work.

But this … this seemed as natural as pigs in shit, 'cause I knew how our bodies worked. I knew what was going to drive them wild with lust for me.

Or maybe wolves to the hunt?

Twenty minutes, a thorough washing by the boys of every square inch of my body like I was some prized king or something, down to such care they expressed over each of my fingers and toes, and then we was all dressed and ready to leave.

I looked sheepishly at all of them, my eyes darting to theirs only to look away because I was too embarrassed about what we'd all done. I knew better to think them thoughts about being some sort of … oh, yeah, never mind.

"Well, uh, be seein' ya, I guess," I said, sounding even dumber than it sounded in my head before I said it.

I was so like a fish out of water with these guys, like a house cat running with the dogs. Who was I kidding here? I so wasn't of their kind. At best, I was a passerby, a lookie-loo to see what I could see. Yeah, well, I saw plenty – and did a helluva lot more.

With *all* of them, too.

Eight boyfriends, when I had only ever wished for one.

"Careful what you wish for … " I could hear Cory say to me.

Yeah, message received, loud and clear.

Eyes firmly aimed at the ground, I started to move off, like a dog with my tail between my legs. I stopped at the door to the gym that lead back outside, and spared a glance at them. They just stood there slack jawed like I'd just slapped them one but good.

"Just where in the *hell* do you think you're goin'?" Riley called out to me.

I stood in the doorway, leaning my back against the door so that a bright shard of light stabbed its way across the floor to where they all stood. Gawd, was they ever beautiful to behold.

"Well, uh, home, I guess. Mama's gonna be lookin' for me, I'm late as it is …"

Riley just looked at the other boys who just shrugged like they all couldn't understand what I'd just said, like I was speaking Greek or something.

"*YOU* ain't goin' anywhere without us. You got that? Not anymore."

And I felt something strong coming from all of them, but mostly from Riley. I may be attached to them all now, but Jesus, Mary and Joseph, did I ever feel like Riley was still calling all the shots.

He slowly came up to me and put his fingers in the loops of my britches and tugged at my hips, shaking me playful like that brought a smile to both our lips.

"We belong to you now, 'member?"

"Well, yeah, I guess …"

"No, guessin' – we's serious, Hank. You better get that through your thick skull, 'cause we ain't playin' around here. This here is some serious shit. Okay, I know what we did don't seem right to ya, on account-a how we've all been brought up and all. But after we became a, well, uh, a team, yeah, a *team*, then it just felt as right as rain to us. I know it did to you, too. You can't fake that, what we did in there." He indicated with a toss of his head behind him the shower area I could still spy in the distance.

He looked at me solemnly. "Wherever you go, we go. That's how it is now. We'll ne'er be far away now."

He tapped the side of his head letting me know that they were still there, inside. I did a quick check and sure 'nuff, they were all there. I could feel each of them. Odd thing was, as my mind and body roamed over them, I could feel them and taste that particular taste of them, as if my body could play it all back at will. Looking at Spike I could feel him course through me. Same for the other boys but with Tanner and Riley it was extra strong. Riley kissed my forehead and ran his hands around my waist.

"C'mon now, we'll walk ya home."

Goddammit, Mama really was gonna shit ...

Cory might smile though.

Why I thought that was though, I just couldn't say.

CHAPTER THREE

The Binding and the Hunt

The walk home was quiet. No one appeared to want to talk anyhow. They kept close. And I know how odd it looked, the nine of us walking down the road and to the other side of town where my family store was and me just walking the bike along with the other boys in tow. The looks we caught as we moved slowly past the other folks in town, the whispers and slightly cocked heads at the absurdity of it wasn't lost upon me.

I wanted to shout, *'twasn't like I was askin' for any of this!*

Though no one heard that on account I didn't say nothing.

So we marched on.

The boys stopped here and there to look at something that'd catch their eye, usually some collection of girls who passed amongst us coming out of the new Dairy Queen in the center of town, until Riley thought they'd lingered enough. He'd snap his fingers and they'd dutifully pull away and follow along.

I turned the corner what led to our store and ran smack into Mrs. Greene. She was a kindly old lady as ever you did meet. She and Cory got along famously, so I always made sure to be extra kind to her.

Only now, surrounded by the gang, I could see her eyes took on a slightly fearful look in my direction. I made sure to put on as bright a smile as I could, nodding gently to her before greeting her.

"Afternoon, Mrs. Greene. Sure is a beautiful afternoon, innit?"

Eyeing Tanner and Riley before, her eyes scanned the rest of the boys who now closed ranks behind me, Her eyes finally found mine as she clutched her grocery poke a little tighter to her withered bosom.

Her eyes narrowed slightly, her smile a little tighter than usual. She nodded just once to me in agreement. I leaned the bike against Spike, who I found had moved in beside me, and took Mrs. Greene gently by her elbow and walked her through the boys who parted at my gaze — at least having the sense God gave them to look sheepishly away at my moving amongst them to guide my companion safely to the other side.

She stopped as soon as we cleared the pack, looked back at them watching the two of us, no one daring to say a word.

She tilted her head briefly in the direction what led away from my boys.

My boys ...

Having taken a step or two in that direction, with me in tow, she thought we were safely from within earshot she at last spoke; her words weren't quite what I thought they'd be.

"Land sakes, child. Why'd you have to go get acquainted with the likes of them? Now there won't be a girl within a stone's throw who won't be gunnin' fer ya now."

She looked back at them, and I saw that it wasn't fear in her eyes, but desire. She was responding to them like a woman should for a virile man, the way things was supposed to be — excepting for her age and all which was a bit off putting even if it was remotely understandable. Her gaze turned slowly back to me even if she lingered on Riley a bit longer than I cared for. I noted that he had started to move toward me. Seeing this, I knew I had to cut our conversation short or things could get a whole mess stickier.

"And that Riley Raintree. Ne'er did I think that I'd find an Injin attractive, but Lawd o'Mercy, that boy is a heap of lovin' on two legs. Ain't he though?"

She broke her eye contact with him and turned to face me, her gaze becoming far more pointed, precision there that cut straight into me.

"But I 'spect you'd know all about that, wouldn'tcha now?"

That sucker-punched me to where I found I couldn't breathe much less have anything to say in response. That seemed to be the signal that Riley was waiting for, 'cause he swooped right in and diverted her attention from my awkward response.

"Naw, Vera, you know you need to get back to John and get his supper goin', now don'tcha? That man's belly ain't goin' wait much longer, ya know. He's worked a hard day at the mine and he's gonna need him a good supper before bed."

He took her elbow from me, leaving me to pant and shake out the willies from my head, even if I did note that he winked at me as he passed. With the profundity of her accusation still ringing in my ears, I could sort of hear him give her gentle pleasantries as he sped her on her way. A second or two later he caught up to me and pulled me along at my elbow.

"You'll have to get used to that, I'm afraid, baby. We sort of bring that out in females." He glanced back over his shoulder at the retreating form of Vera Greene. He chuckled.

"Regardless of their age."

I looked sideways at him, a gentle smirk playing across his face. The bastard was really enjoying my being flustered by what Vera had said.

"Ain't like that will ever happen, not since I've had you. I suspect it'll be like that with all the boys now," he whispered as we moved back amongst the boys. "There's just something diff'rent 'bout bein' with a boy like you, Hank. Does somethin' to a man."

As I got up to where Spike could hand my bike back to me, he ruffled my hair, and winked while Riley took point with Tanner not too far behind, followed by me and Spike and the others bringing up the rear. Our pack moved on.

I took my bike around the side of the store to the door that led to the basement, brought it inside and rested it against the wall just inside the door. The boys followed me in and we all sort of milled about the stock. Darby and Dylan took an interest in some of the canned goods while Riley moved slowly across the floor to the shower on the other side of the building. He approached the curtain and ran his hand along it, before leaning in and sniffing at it. He paused and turned his head looking at me with a wicked gaze to him.

"Well, now, who do we have here?" Cory's voice rang from the top of the stairs.

The boys seemed to know her before they seen her. They all moved to the staircase what was in the center of the large basement and stood in that shaft of light that pierced the semi-darkness, bathing them all in a certain magical glow.

"Howdy, Miss Cora," they all seemed to say in unison.

"Hi there, boys. Y'all walk our Hank back from school, now didja? Well, that was mighty nice of you. Can't say why you all haven't done that before. Seems right to watch over him now, don't it?"

My mouth went sorta slack-jawed at her words, talking to them like they'd known each other and socialized over the years when I know'd deep down that that had never happened.

The boys looked up at her with nothing short of admiration and respect, as if she were the mother to them all.

I started to move from Riley to where the other boys had gathered and looked up at Cory. "Sorry, Cory. I know I shoulda said I wasn't comin' home alone. Only we didn't plan this out. It just sorta happened. Where's Mama?"

She smiled warmly though I couldn't say it was entirely for me, but more for the boys what was standing around me when she spoke next.

"Your Ma is havin' herself one of her quiet spells. She's upstairs restin'. It'll just be the ..." she trailed off, a gentle turn of her head as if she knew all along that Riley and Tanner weren't too far off.

When she took a step or two down the stairs she spied them slowly approaching to where I stood. Riley slowly slipped a gentle hand around my waist which shocked me something fierce and I thought I was gonna have me a fainting spell right on the spot. But when I turned to Cory she just beamed like everything was right on track like they was supposed to be.

Now, how in the hell could that be?

But there she was, grinning and smiling like what Riley was doing was the best thing she coulda ever laid eyes on.

"I knew you boys would eventually click. Y'all hungry? I had a feelin' in the pit of my stomach that Hank wasn't gonna be alone today. Why don't you boys come upstairs and I can make us somethin' to eat in the back?"

The boys didn't need to be told twice. They all glanced at one another. Their eyes sparked up like they'd won a million dollars or something and lit up them damned stairs like their britches was on fire.

Cory just chuckled and took the lead up to the main part of the store.

I, on the other hand, shrugged hard out of Riley's grasp and rounded on him like he'd lost his ever cotton-picking mind.

"What'd you go and do that fer? Cory saw that. You just get all bone dead stupid on me? She's gonna tell Mama!"

Riley shot a look at Tanner that only had a certain amount of glee in it – like they was in on some secret kinda club and even Cory was a member but I sure as hell wasn't and I didn't like it one dang bit, no siree.

"Yeah, you all keep smilin' like you're doin'. Leave me outta it why don'tcha?"

That miserable whine crept back into my voice again but I couldn't help how hopeless and floundering I was feeling.

Riley pulled me around to him and tugged me in tight.

"Now, who do ya think told us that we needed to pay more attention to ya, that your time had finally come? That we was ready fer ya? Hmm?" He practically hummed with the pleasure he was feeling at that final reveal – and I knew, I just knew that he was talking about my Cory.

Cory?

I just couldn't wrap my mind around it.

Tanner came around and stood on the other side of me and I was nestled between them. When we got like this the only thing that became clear to me was that I lost all sense of reason. And don't think for a second that the irony of that situation wasn't lost upon me. They just had that way of making my brain get all foggy like on a dewy morning. Tanner leaned down a bit and kissed the top of my head, while Riley leaned forward and kissed the tip of my nose. I never did feel anything of the kind in what was going through my head and body just then. I sighed, somewhat contentedly.

"Well, we better git upstairs or the boys'll finish whatever it is Cory's gonna wrestle up for us."

They released me and I started to climb the stairs when something in the air shifted. A smell I never did smell before came waffling down the staircase. Riley was in front of me on the stairs so danged fast the air from his movement nearly knocked me over.

We froze for a moment, listening intently at the sounds of footsteps above when Ry and Tanner emitted a low growl in their throats and I could only feel one thing coursing through me: my boys was *angry*.

The air at the top of the stairs was thick with the smell of bacon and tension. Not the two of the best smells to put together. For some reason I couldn't figure out, I could literally smell it too. 'Twas a tangy smell – like wet fur or a man who hadn't showered – pungent and definitively male.

Problem was, 'twasn't anyone in the store other than my boys – *my boys*, I still was getting used to that – surrounding Cory who was grilling them up something as a hearty snack. Everyone seemed to freeze like one of them Norman Rockwell pictures you'd see every now and then on *Life* magazine.

Along with the tang of tension, the smell of bacon and potatoes filled the air. The sizzle from the stove top along the back of the large store was crackling and popping with the bacon grease that was frying up the potatoes. I could just tell by the smell that they were nearly done, too. How did I know that all of a sudden? I can' t say, but I did.

But it was that pungent tang in the air that had left me with a bad feeling and my boys hackles were all up about it. A few guttural growls rumbled in their chests. Tanner moved in front of me and Riley moved even further beyond him.

I spared a glance back at Cory and she, too, stood there, though she was busy eyeing how the boys whole demeanor had changed.

"Hank, you better get over here, son," she said softly, waving her hand to beckon me to her. I looked back at Riley who turned slightly in our direction and nodded to Tanner and me just once. Something muffled passed betwixt them all that I couldn't quite make out, like we was talking on the telephone but with something covering the mouthpiece. I knew they were speaking to one another but it was like it was behind a closed door. I couldn't quite make out what was being said.

"Hank, you better do what Cory says," Tanner whispered, starting to push me gently in her direction past the other boys.

I just didn't know what to think. I mean I was the man of the house and store, and yet my boys were all up in arms about something that I could only smell in the air. I didn't want to leave Tanner's or Riley's side. But the other boys had started to move toward Tanner and Riley – regrouping as they came forward, each placed a gentle but forceful hand prodding me back to Cory's safe grasp.

Her hands were soft but surprisingly firm. She whipped my focus around so I had to look at her. Her gaze was pointed and held none of that softness and motherly look about them. She was about as sharp as the boys were.

"Now you listen here, Hank. I want you to git yourself upstairs with your Mama. She's out cold 'cause I gave her something to calm herself. It's better you stay up there with her while we take care of this."

I looked quickly at my boys – goddamn it they were supposed to be *my boys* and here was Cory telling me to put my tail betwixt my legs and hide. Well, there ain't no way I was gonna do that. Cory was one step ahead of me.

"Henry Callum O'Malley, now you git upstairs and see to your mama like I told you. The boys and I'll take care of what needs tendin' to here." Her hand became vice-like as she pulled me along the length of the back kitchen and along to the back stairs – out of eyesight of my boys.

She turned me on the spot at the bottom of the staircase. I could just peer around the long back wall and could sort of see Riley at the open double front doors, his body was taut like he wanted to spring from the front veranda and shred whatever or whoever was coming our way.

"But ..."

"Not another danged word, Hank. You git or I'll give ya something to git on about, ya hear? I've got real work to do here with Riley and the boys; you'll be a distraction. Let us handle this and see to your ma! Now git!"

A low rumble from my boys' chests said whatever the fuck this was, it was bad and it was near.

Run ... Tanner uttered in my head.

Git upstairs, Hank ... Mike barked a bit louder than Tanner.

Baby, you need to get up there like she says ... do it for me, for us? I can't watch out fer ya and keep things settled – I need you safe. DO IT NOW! Riley said so forcefully in my head that I turned and dashed up the stairs before I knew what was happening, like he was there and was pulling me to him — only it was just me.

I dashed into Mama's bedroom, and with the slam of the door I turned slowly to take in the room. It was dark with the curtains drawn. Only a single table lamp next to the bed provided any light in the room. It was quiet, too, like she was dead to the world. A funereal setting. She lay there, dressed in a long black shift, in the middle of her bed, arms crossed gently over her bosom, her hand clutching at something I couldn't see, only that it was on some sort of delicate chain I never did see before.

But I didn't have time to deal with any of that. In the quiet of the room I could hear Cory's voice along with another man's. I could suddenly feel my boys circling this newcomer in our store. That smell, that pungent and tangy smell, it was definitely from him. The air was so thick with it that I almost wretched.

I stood at one of the large windows and pulled the curtain slightly open. A shard of light cut across my face. I glanced down to the front of the store at ground level. I spied a couple of men standing just off the front porch – big guys they was too and I didn't recognize either of them. They looked none too happy to be here neither, the way they kept looking about theyselves, like they was gonna get jumped by somebody but quick. Excitement, and not in a good way, hung in the air like a foul stench. Whatever this was, it was bad; of that there was no mistaking.

I could hear some voices raised downstairs. I tried to listen in on my little connection between me and the boys but found I couldn't. It was like I was behind a thick glass or something. I was cut-off, trapped.

In my trying to listen for my boys I found I heard something else. Some low murmur played upon my ears. Something sounded both familiar and foreign all at the same time. I slowly pulled away from the curtain, letting it fall back into place, blocking what little bright light there was at this point yet, somehow, just like when I was in the showers, I could see perfectly well.

It was then I realized that what was familiar about this sound was that, mingled with others, I could clearly make out my mother's voice. I slowly moved toward her bed where she laid completely still. As I got closer I saw her lips barely moving – repeating something over and over – gently, as if she were at Mass and saying her rosary. Only she 'twasn't holding a rosary.

As I leaned over her to see what it was she was saying, I noticed that the chain wrapped around her slender hand, her fist was clenched tightly, almost to the point where it shook with such determination. It was then that I realized what she was doing.

'Tweren't *prayers* she was saying.

She was *castin'* ...

Since I couldn't feel any of my boys, I panicked. I bolted for the door to my mama's room only to find I couldn't grip the knob with any force to turn it, like 'twas covered in grease or something. I yanked on it anyway and the door wouldn't budge. It may as well been tacked to a brick wall for the good it was doing to pull upon it.

The room began to hum. It was low and I felt it in the pit of my belly way before I heard it. With it, all of the air seemed to become still. 'Twas as if I were plunged into the river, immersed and completely lost to my surroundings.

MAMA! I screamed inside, calling for her to no avail.

She couldn't or wouldn't hear me. My mouth opened, equal parts slack and twisted in pain as the darkness descended. The air was thick; moving became hard. I struggled against it. Slowly my knees came into contact with the floor. I thought that was the worst of it. I didn't know how wrong I was about that.

Words, whispers as if there were suddenly many people in the room with words coming at me from all sides. Words that I couldn't make out, coming so fast and furious they were hard to understand. Words, solid and heavy, they were. From all sides they pressed in on me. I buckled under their weight. I tried to call out – to cry out with my mind to Riley.

Panic ...

Fear ...

I couldn't feel them. *They were there a moment ago* ...

Inwardly I scrambled; I pushed hard against the tide. It was hard, really hard to do that. Like the weight of the world was suddenly on my shoulders, I screamed under the pressure only there was no sound but the whispers. Those words, they grew louder the harder I pushed. The floor began to buckle; a rumble began to form in my chest. The weight of the room began to lessen 'til that rumble became a rage. It built and fell back upon itself, rattling walls and windows alike.

My boys ...

They are MINE!

The fire inside of me built – a rage that my boys were missing – like my hands were moving in the dark I reached out to them with my mind.

Nothin' will have my boys ...

Nothin'!

The hum grew louder, matching the volume of my roar, like breaking the surface of the river I finally found my voice. The entire room became bright with light, hard brilliant white light, like I was staring into the sun. Only it didn't hurt, but it was powerful with the warmth it radiated.

And it was strong ...

The building shook with it. I turned to look at my mother. The whispering voices rose to a chorus, bellowing broadly, pushing back against me. I roared – glass shattered somewhere in the room. I could hear the pieces fall to the ground behind me. I took a step and felt the floor buckle.

The building shook to the foundation ...

My body raged. I felt parts of me grow. Muscles and bone. Sharp spikes of pain, followed immediately with euphoria. A bliss to each break. My face hurt all over. My mouth felt this tremendous pull, as if something was tugging on it something fierce. My shirt tore from me. Bones cracked. I hurt all over, my rage soon turned to a cry. 'Twas like a switch suddenly got flipped. The world snapped back into place, like the fury of a tornado that silence pulled around me, taking what strength I'd been building with it. The pain was overwhelming. Everything went from white to red to black. I collapsed, fell into darkness. As I felt my body fall to the floor I could hear a commotion, a running of feet and calls and barking. Noise – so much noise.

Why'd there have to be so much danged noise?

As I began to fall it all felt strange.

As if I were falling ...

... *up.*

Water.

I was moving in water, yet I could breathe.

The water was thick ... like 'twas made of syrup.

Soft lips on my forehead.

Heated breath.

A deep growl softly murmured. A man's voice.

Home.

Hearth.

Him ...

Inside that well of darkness I pulled myself from sleep. I clawed inwardly in the blackness, swimming against that current, striving to get me to the surface again. My eyes slowly opened, blurred and out of focus, but finding myself in the bathtub of our bathroom. A gentle hand to my forehead, though far larger than my mother's or Cory's.

The water was warm, but not unbearably so. I tried to look above me to see who was in the room with me but found I really couldn't move my head.

I began to struggle, a short grunt burst from my lips.

The door opened and I could just catch it out of the corner of my eye.

The hand on my forehead retreated. I sprang up from the end of the tub in a flurry of thick water and wild movement. I turned to whomever had entered the room, wiping the hair from my forehead.

When I succeeded pulling the hair from my face I found no one in the room at all but myself.

Someone was here. I know'd it. I felt it.

No one.

The water was like syrup along my skin, like the raw whites of an egg, like I was emerging from something, a birth of sorts.

I slipped from the tub, feeling my feet underneath me seemed to have a new meaning. Whatever was in the tub with me was slick, yet I found my feet were solid and true. I reached out with my mind, trying once again to find my boys. They came back to me in rapid succession, like the pelting from a tommy gun. They were that fast in responding.

?! Darby – filled with shock, came to me first.

?! Toby.

?! Maynard.

They were there ... populating my head and heart, like little bursts of light and warmth. The feeling they was generating was bringing feeling back into me.

?!   *?!* (Dylan and Mike, one never far from one another)

?! Spike

!! (That'd be Tanner)

!!!! There was Riley. Thank the maker! Jesus, I don't know what I'd do if I lost him.

There was a patter of feet up the stairs. I could feel Riley easily took two to three steps at a time. Just how many I wasn't sure, as my head was a tad foggy yet. They were just yammering at me a mash of words from each of them. But one thing was clear: relief.

Okay, two things ...

Relief and love. So much love.

I prepared to move to get myself a towel but I faltered. I slipped and fell to one knee in a loud crack. I winced.

"Not as nimble as I thought ..."

I placed a hand gingerly upon the side of the tub as they bounded through the door. Riley was at my side followed by Tanner and the others.

"I'm fine ... FINE! I tell you," I barked a bit louder than I intended. This seemed to have the effect of keeping all of them from rushing me. Tanner and Riley placed their big strong hands under each of my arms.

They helped me to my feet but allowed me to stand on my own. Part of me was only slightly embarrassed at being so exposed with them, naked and slick with that syrupy mess what I laid in. I still couldn't get over that I had eight boyfriends now. It was a bit much to sort through. But there was no doubt, they were all mine, each one coursing through me and the pull upon my heart from each of them was strong.

"Just help me to bed, will you?"

"You can't, babe. I need to get you cleaned up first," Riley said softly, his hand to my lower back which I noted had slipped slightly so his hand could embrace my ass. I didn't mind. They were here to take care of me. My body was as much theirs as it was my own. Somehow I just knew that was the way things were now. They may say they were mine, but I could just tell my body, my heart was their'n too.

I looked over my shoulder at what mess 'twas in the tub. It would take a solid week of scrubbing just to get that to working order again.

"There was no way *anything* was ever gonna get clean in that again, for at least a week," I mumbled to them all.

We all looked at it again. I could feel the guys look around us at the disaster that used to resemble our tub.

"Or maybe ever," Riley said flatly. The guys had a chuckle at that one. I did too, just a bit. Then I realized that it was probably me who was gonna have to do the cleaning.

Riley scooped me up into his arms with little notice. I yelped at how fast it all happened.

"Spike, get him somethin' to change into, will ya?"

"You get him somethin' and let me take him down."

Spike started to move toward me but Tanner growled darkly and Spike suddenly thought differently. He scowled the tiniest bit but then moved off to do as he was told.

"Mike, go down and make sure that no one is in the store where they can see us bringing him down. Scare 'em off if you have to. You know what to do."

Without another word he was gone. There was dedication, I thought.

"Well, no time like the present, right?"

"Yeah, and the sooner the better, 'cause you're usually just sex on two legs to us but, uh," he wrinkled his nose and made a scrunched up face, "just not right now."

I looked around at the boys and they all were making a similar face.

I sniffed myself a tiny bit. I don't know how I missed it earlier. It wasn't just awful smelling; it was just plain foul.

"Ah, Christ, get my ass downstairs quick. Why didn'tcha all tell me sooner? I smell like I've been in with the pigs in ways ..." I sniffed myself again along my shoulder, "yeah, ways I just think ain't right."

They all laughed and Riley carried me out. As we got to the top of the staircase I noticed that the back double window was thrown wide open, which was odd for an autumn day like today which had grown to be a bit gloomy with the coming of evening. I was about to ask about it when a whistle came up from down below. Before I could say anything further, Riley took to the window at a full run and we leapt through it, only a second later to land firmly, but far softer than I would've thought imaginable as his feet made contact with the soft earth that ran along the back of the hillside that abutted our building. From there I could see Mike at the far corner with an eye to the town that lay beyond. He signaled that all was well and the boys what leapt from the window started to move off to meet Mike and slip around the corner and into the basement. Riley turned his head to me, his big brown eyes drinking me in. I knew I was a mess, not much to look at.

I'll always wanna look at you, Hank. You's the purdiest man I ever did see, he cooed into my head. Before I could say anything he nuzzled my wet nose with his.

"Okay if I set you down now?"

"You coulda set me down earlier. You didn't need to do that. I was perfectly capable of walking downstairs on my own, ya know."

"So shoot me for wantin' my hands all over you, then. 'Sides, I don't know that I want you paradin' that muscled body around just anyone. We may belong to you now, but dammit, the pack *will* defend what's ours."

He raised a brow with that sexy smirk that never failed to get to my manly parts. It wasn't failing now. This only made that smirk take hold and blossom across his face. Lawdy, was he a beautiful sight. He sighed, breathing me in again, forgetting for the moment just how awful I smelled.

"But you're right. You need to get cleaned up some."

He set me down and I leaned forward and smelled him. The slime that covered my body had left him a sticky mess too. My feet were already tracking leaves and pine needles as it was.

"You know you're gonna have to get cleaned up some too. You got me all over ya, and, uh, okay, I am beginnin' to see how you planned this all out ahead o'time, smart boy that you are."

He chuckled, placing a possessive hand on my ass again to guide me to the corner of the building. I casually slipped around the open door and into the basement.

"So, what was that stuff I was in up there? And where's Mama an' Cory? And what happened in the store when all that stuff was goin' on? I heard shoutin' and some movement and then ..."

I stopped, turned slowly to find Riley peeling himself out of his clothes. Tanner was right behind him, taking them from him.

"Shower first," Tanner said, with a head nudge toward the stall at the end of the basement, "then we'll meet yer Ma and Miss Cory upstairs where they's waitin' to talk."

"Boys, a little privacy please?" Riley said in a flat tone.

The boys moved slowly but purposefully up the stairs as Riley handed the last of his clothes to Tanner who took them and started to walk past me but stopped and placed a finger under my chin, wrinkled his nose a bit but leaned in to kiss me anyhow. I let him drink from my mouth for a few before he pulled back and chuckled nodding again toward the shower.

"Git," was all he said as he started to ascend the stairs.

"I'll send some clothes down for ya both."

And with that we were alone, Riley and me naked, the lust between us growing without so much as a word or thought to push it along, despite what a mess I was.

He kissed me softly as he nudged me gently but purposefully toward the shower. A moment or so later we were under the water and the feeling of that syrup mess falling away was like I'd imaged a butterfly breaking from its cocoon. 'Twas freeing, so incredibly freeing.

Riley ran his hands all over me, everywhere he could get. We kissed as his large rough hands moved across my skin, ensuring that what gunk there was had gone down the drain. His mouth found mine next, and he kept murmuring between nips, bites and the scorch of his mouth moving across my skin – in nearly every place he could, making me understand that I was a part of them now.

He spent a great deal of time sucking upon me, laving his tongue along my shaft and head, teasing me to where I thought I'd go out of my fucking mind with all the sensations he was plying on me.

"Riley, I'm close ..."

His hands came up to grip one ass cheek in each, kneading them to where I thought I'd have bruises. I knew what they'd all said that they were mine. But deep down inside I knew really t'was the other way around. My body, heart and soul were their'n. 'Tis the way 'tis, thassall.

Riley growled deeply, low and very much like an animal. Somewhere I could feel the other boys listening in. I didn't mind, except I thought it might make for an embarrassing situation should they be around others so I gently but resolutely closed them all off. I could feel their disappointment – from what I could tell from Tanner – the sex was a communal thing with us. But I wanted Riley to myself just now. They'd all have to wait their turn. Just before I shut myself to them I let them all know how much I was looking forward to spending time with each of them, or all of them. That seemed to appease as I let them all go into the darkness of my thoughts.

Riley's mouth was a sin, plain and simple. Its velvety smoothness, so wet, warm and inviting made me never want to leave. He purred as I pressed to the back of his throat. A couple of more thrusts and the middle finger of his right hand pressed into me. He massaged me as he continued to pull upon my loins. A second or two later and the first finger was followed by a second, opening me, giving me their all. With that sensation I couldn't hold back any longer and I let go in a torrent of emotion and fluid that felt like he was draining me of all life itself. I poured myself into him and he drank, like a parched man coming out of the desert into an oasis. I slipped from his mouth, and his hands retreated from their assault of me as he slowly stood up. He kissed me, only then did I realize that he hadn't consumed much of me at all. It was sweet and salty – I'd tasted it before when I'd relieved the morning wood at times in my bed alone.

Alone.

I wasn't ever gonna be alone again. That's what they'd said. I was beginning to believe them. He pulled back, so much of me still on our lips and tongues. He smiled softly, his eyes looking deep within my own. Chocolate brown they was. So dark and beautiful. I wanted to swim in them forever, I did.

"Hank O'Malley, ne'er in a million years did I think you'd ever come to me like you did. There is so much I've gotta show ya."

We kissed for a bit. I felt him reach around me for the bar of soap on the small shelf. As we kissed, he began to lather my body. He broke it off as he turned me to face the shower head so the water could pour down my backside. I felt him press between me.

"Oh, yes, Riley. Please."

He chuckled softly. It was the sexiest sound I ever did hear, that soft chuckle was. There was so much buried inside of it and I'll be danged if how any of what had happened between us came to pass. It was a mystery, plain and simple. They had a lot of explaining to do, that was for sure.

"Mmm-hmm," he murmured as I felt him lather his cock generously. Never in all my life did I think that Riley Raintree and me would be anything but distant acquaintances. Passing friends, at best. Distant enemies, at worst.

He thrust into me in one long torturous move. I sighed as he pulled me to him.

"That ain't *ever*," he pulled out and back into me hard, "gonna," another fierce and hard thrust, "happen ... We are yours. You have our lives in your hands now, lover boy. You have our hearts," he whispered into my ear as he buried himself deep within, circling his hips in a way what made me hitch my breath with such an intensity that it brought me to my toes, his fucking did.

"Now," his voice became gravel-like with lust, "open up and let me do what you're achin' for me to do."

His breath was like a blast from the furnace on my face, scorching across my ear, making me clench uncontrollably around his cock. He shuddered when I did that to him.

"Ahhhh-gh, sssst, that's it, baby. I know what you need. You keep sayin' it over and over to all of us. Two nights from now, you're going to go ravenous for it. It's the time of bindin', where we officially become a pack. The sexin' of it – the way you're gonna claim each of us to you will be unbreakable. Each boy," he ground himself in that circular motion deep within me that made my knees buckle a bit from it all. I bit my lip as he continued to tell me how it was gonna be, and I wanted it. I wanted it all. "Each boy is layin' his life before you. He will pledge his life to you, seed you with it, bind himself to you in ways that can destroy him if you ever repudiate him. Each boy knows what's ahead, what that means.

That's what I mean when I say *we belong to you!*"

He slammed into me hard, circling within again, making me yelp with desire for more, biting my bottom lip to hold it back. I liked it when he hurt me deep inside, made me quake and want him more. I could feel him coursing through me, mind and body – his thoughts, his feelings, everything that he is was pouring into me.

A guttural growl began to form in my throat. It did it all on its own. I felt my body flush, bone started to snap, the pain was intense but deeply alluring. I wanted more.

"More!" I began to thrust back onto him, taking possession of him.

"Yes!"

"More ... Give ... Me ... More!"

I knew I was fucking myself onto him hard. He braced himself as best he could and held his ground while I took. I heard cracks going on inside my body. Things weren't right. I know they weren't, but it never felt so right in my whole life. It was that feeling of being of two minds. One consumed my thoughts, what I know'd to be right by what people said 'twas. Then there was the one of my body; it ached. It craved. It *wanted, desired, fed* on my boys.

"My! Boys!"

"Yes! Take it, ah baby. It's yours; take it from me!"

He was practically begging then he met me thrust for thrust as I devoured him — he burst, like a shower directly into my soul and I roared. My own juices splayed out in front of me, painting the shower wall with the biggest danged load of cum I ever did see. My hands shot out onto the wall and I saw my hands were bigger than they were before, with claws instead of my usual nails though my vision was obscured by the water from the shower. With a shake of my head things seemed to return to normal. I was panting with how much he was feeding me. It seemed to go on and on. And it was the most glorious feeling, I can tell you. He leaned forward and bit me hard along my shoulder, but not so much as to pierce the skin this time, just enough to reclaim what he knew deep inside was his and his alone.

Best.

Fucking.

Feeling.

Ever!

How long we were there, I can't say. Nor could I say when everything had gone back to being their normal self. My hands were once again my hands. It seemed all like a strange dream that I couldn't fully escape. It seemed time had stopped. I could feel each water droplet from that shower head, suspended in air in that moment. I could see all of it frozen, like I alone could move within the space between one second and the next.

And in that I heard something that chilled my heart to the bone. I slowly turned my head to find that Riley was still frozen in that last moment of our union. But we weren't alone. Not by a long shot. It seemed to be everywhere and nowhere all at the same time. It was a low and dark laugh. A laugh with no mirth in it. That there was evil. It was what Mama'd call malevolent, and the worst part was, it was ravenous. And I could just tell by the way it was watching us, 'tweren't no good. When at last it spoke, it was as if hell itself had opened up and Lucifer hisself was calling to me. It said one word to me and one word only ...

"Soon ..."

CHAPTER FOUR

Call of the Wild

Like the snap of a rubber band, the world came back into place.

When everything came back to normal, Riley acted like nothing had happened at all. I didn't know what to think. I tried to pass it off like I'd imagined it all. So I didn't say nothing. I mean, all of this was so danged new and I really didn't know much to begin with.

As we got dressed with the clothes what were brought down from my room, I began to take stock in what I did know. 'Tweren't much, that I can tell you. But I counted them all off in my head anyhow:

1. The boys really were some sort of pack, though why that was I didn't rightly know, and if I thought on it too much it made my head hurt. So I didn't.

2. Cory seemed to know them and they acted like they knew her too, like they was communicating all along or something –

which was beyond ludicrous, wasn't it?

3.   While I was the one who'd be bedding the boys, it seemed that
     in some real way Riley was right, they did belong to me. That
     part was definitely true – despite how much I tried to apply it
     the other way around. They were mine. And it wasn't lost on me
     that what Riley told me about being able to destroy them if I cast
     one of them out; I knew it to be true. I could feel it.

4.   And speaking of *castin'* … what the *fuck* was up with Mama?

While I was able to process most of it, there were things that I
couldn't figure out at all. For one, what was up with my clothes being all
tight and constricting like? When had that happened? I mean, it wasn't
like they all of a sudden didn't fit, but it sure was plain as the nose on my
face that I'd grown some in the span of one afternoon. Riley just looked at
me with a renewed interest. He couldn't keep his hands or his lips off me.
He was like a giddy school girl who got her way with a boy and he just
couldn't believe it was happening unless his mouth or some other part of
him was touching on me. It was nice but it was also very, very strange, like
our loving had made him loopy or drunk somehow. It made me wonder
what was going to happen to Spike when I was with him. He was already
loopy for me.

I finally convinced Riley to release me enough so we could navigate
the stairs to the main floor of the store. It was closed up for the night.
Some of the boys were putting stuff back on shelves, while a few more was
sweeping up some feed that had been spilt. Mama wasn't gonna be happy
about that. Speaking of …

"Where's Mama?"

I looked around a bit more and noticed that Cory weren't around
neither.

"And where's Cory? Cory! Mama!"

Tanner came up to me quickly with both his hands up as if to stall me in my quest to find them. I know I gave him a look like he'd lost his ever-loving mind, only 'cause I was, but didn't stop him in the least in reaching out for me, his big paws on either shoulder.

"Now, you listen here, Hank O'Malley. Your Ma and Cory, well, they know what's goin' on here far more than most of us. When you collapsed like you did upstairs, Cory and your mama knew just what to do. They got us to git you into the tub right quick while they was preparin' that special bath you was in, see?"

"NO! Tan, I don't see. I don't see a helluva lotta things goin' on around here! You all are keepin' secrets. Secrets, and half-truths, and stuff that concerns me but, oh, hell no, we can't go tellin' Hank cause he'll just fall apart, now won't he?"

I rounded on Riley, just as pointed and biting as I knew how. 'Twasn't fair, I know, but I was more pissed off than a cornered 'coon, I can tell you that. I really didn't care whose feelings I was trampling on just then. They all needed to come clean and tell me what the fuck was going on with me – *and* with all of them!

"No, instead," I poked a hard finger in Ry's chest, making him cringe the tiniest bit as he backed away from me with each poke, his eyes wide like I was plum crazy. Which, come to think of it, I sorta was. But therein was the whole crux of my problem and I needed to get to the bottom of it all. "Instead, you all treat me like I was made of glass or somethin'. Like I was the village idiot what needed constant tendin' to or I'd fall down and get a boo-boo or somethin'. Hell, I dunno. You keep tellin' me that all this..."

I waved my hand around to all of them who had slowly made their way to where I was at the front of the store, followed by an equally wild waving of said hands around like I *was* the village idiot. I needed to get a hold of myself and be more of a man about it all. Just what that *all* was though was the greatest mystery and I wanted it solved. Right. Fuckin'. Now!

"This is supposed to be special. That what we got?"

I pointed to each one of them making them jump back like I was a big ol' bee and I was stinging the hell outta them.

"That we need to treat it with care and how we's all are re-writin' the rules or some danged thing and yet no one, not a GODDAMNED one of ya will tell me what the FUCK we're talkin' about! I want answers GODDAMMIT and I want them NOW!"

The front door behind me slammed shut, startling me and making me spin around to find Mama and Cory standing there – Mama had on her calm face, which was the face I used to get just before she'd take into whooping me but good. Cory, on the other hand, was trying like hell to stifle a laugh.

"You want answers, is that it, then?" she said very quiet-like — another bad sign, I was sure. "Well, Hank," She raised a brow and I knew my ass was well and truly cooked; she was gonna give it to me all right. "I think you're right. You're old enough now to know what happened."

"Ruth ... you sure now?" Cory asked her with a gentle hand to my mother's arm.

My mother cocked her head slightly to her right to eye Cory directly.

"Yes, it's time Hank knew it all – about this town, its history, how the menfolk have been cursed by us. *All of it.*"

"Even ... ?"

"Yes, even 'bout his daddy. All of it. Forewarned is forearmed. He's been in the dark for far too long."

Then she moved closer to me, her hands going up to the sides of my face, she leaned forward and placed a soft kiss on my forehead.

"But I suppose that was my fault. I was just your mama tryin' to do her level best to keep you safe, Hank. Hopin' against all hope that you'd escape all of this. But it's clear to me after today you can't. In fact, you aren't just involved, you've become my worst nightmare. You are in the center of it all."

I couldn't breathe with each word she'd said. The room started to move about me like that new Hitchcock picture Mama and I went and saw a couple of months back where that guy had vertigo and there was that rush with the camera and the pulling back all at the same time – only I wasn't high up or nothing. So it didn't make no kinda sense. But it was like life itself was being slowly leeched from me. I know I lost color in my face because I could feel my blood pull away.

Tanner and the boys moved quickly in. Tanner had me in his arms holding me up. He placed a soft kiss on my head.

"We gotcha, Hank. We all gotcha. And we ain't ever gonna letcha go, you hear me?"

I slowly took my eyes from Mama and Cory and turned it slightly to see Tanner looking at me with such love and devotion that I knew he meant it all. I slowly started to take them all in. Every boy, every single one of them was looking the same way at me as Tanner was, like they was of a like mind, like we was all one.

"We are," Riley said as he reached me.

Oh yeah, the head thing.

They all nodded slowly, 'cause we were all connected or something. But then it occurred to me – if they could hear me then ... why couldn't I just ... ?

"No, Hank!" Riley said, his head turned to my mother and Cory who seemed to realize what I was starting to put together in my head.

"Boys! Lockdown! Now!"

As soon as he said it the boys collapsed on the spot out cold and fell to the ground. Only Riley and Tanner remained standing. Mama and Cory reached me and gently pried me away from Tanner, leading me to the back of the store to the kitchen and dining table that were tucked behind a great wall partition that separated the register area from where we ate.

I could hear Riley and Tanner slowly rouse the boys with mumbles about *how long was Hank gonna be kept out of things*, and *why'd it take so damned long to get it all out in the open anyway*, and *why didn't we do this sooner* being passed back and forth between them.

I spared a glance behind me as Mama led me to the dining table and indicated I should sit down where Daddy used to sit, making me stop cold in my tracks. No one ever sat in that chair since he left it. It was sort of a place of honor to have that chair there – like we were expecting him to come back or something. Not like that was ever gonna happen, 'cause even I know'd there was no coming back from the dead. Only now, as I realized how far away from the world as I knew it this all was, there was simply no way I could say with any confidence that even Daddy not coming back from the dead was a foregone conclusion. It seemed a great many things were on the table just now.

I stopped just short of sitting in it. It was just a chair for Chrissake; wasn't like it was gonna bite me or nothing. I was being ridiculous, *wasn't I?* Only, it just didn't seem right. That chair remaining empty was a sign of hope, however fleeting or nonsensical it seemed. If'n I sat in it, wasn't I abandoning hope that he'd ever come home? Mama berated me as she watched the dilemma over my absent father play across my face.

"Henry Callum O'Malley, it's just a danged chair." She leaned in with her index finger pointing to that spot on the table that would be his.

"He'd want you to take over for him while he's not here. Now, I know you and I had an unspoken agreement 'bout it remainin' unclaimed. Yeah, well, you're head of this house now. Hell, soon enough, you'll be head of this town, so takin' your daddy's chair is the least of your worries right now. So sit'cha butt down and listen fer what Cory and I have to tell y'all. Hear?"

She looked around at the boys who all sort of nodded as if they were being scolded by her too. We all were looking a might sheepish to tell ya the truth. Me prolly most of all.

Me, taking Daddy's place ...

Just didn't seem like it was right. I still had memories of him sitting there big as life and as warm as a hot day in July. Sometimes I'd sit on his lap while we even ate supper. I'd eat from his plate right along with him. Mama'd just pile enough on the plate for the both of us. His eyes were just as bright and blue like the prettiest danged day you'd ever see. My daddy meant everything to me. Losing him sucked so much life outta me. I was ne'er the same since.

I took a deep, controlled breath. I let it out and slowly slipped into his seat.

I'd like to say it was just a chair, but something inside trembled. Something inside said it 'twasn't my place, like I was just keeping it warm for when he'd come back to me.

And then I smelled him. A soft caress. Big hands, rough from hard work but as gentle as a flower's petal they was whenever he had me. He was strong too. A mountain of a man everyone said. He was monumental to me, bigger 'n life. My daddy was nothing short of God to me. He was God hisself here on Earth. Whate'er he told me to do, that's what I did. No questions asked.

"You know that one day soon, boy, life's gonna try to kick you down, 'n

kick you hard," he'd said one afternoon while he and I was comin' back from a day of fishin' at the creek. "But you ain't ever got a worry if'n I's around to sort it out wit'cha. You got me?"

"Yessum, Pa," I said, proud of the love I could just feel pourin' off of him with those words.

He stopped me, squatted down so he was eye level with me, his bright blues meetin' my own. Gosh a mighty, he was magical, he was. And he was my daddy. And I was from him.

"Now listen here, son. You and me," he indicated the two of us with a finger from his large hand moving slowly between us, "well, we're gonna have some amazin' times ahead. You'll see, boy. There ain't a father n' son more closer built than we are. Ya hear?"

I nodded, wide-eyed and just takin' anything he said as law. My daddy never lied to me, never kept things from me that I needed knowin'. I knew that more than I know'd my own name.

"You're my whole world, son. Everythin' I do, I do for you now."

I tried like hell to make him proud of me. I just beamed and looked him straight in the eye. Well, as much as any five year old could and mean it.

"And I'll do anythin' you ask of me, Pa. 'Cause I's your boy, and you ain't ever goin' ta steer me wrong, right?"

He ruffled the hair on my head even though he know'd just how much it got me goin' before he pulled me so tight to him I thought I'd become a part of him forever. I'da been okay with that. Just me n' him. Well, I guess there'd be Mama too.

Mama.

She just looked at me for a moment while I sat there remembering that day so long ago. Over ten years now. Just didn't seem possible somehow. My eyes darted to hers, which narrowed a tiny bit as if she were trying to decide what was going on in my head just then. I wondered for a moment if she could.

Riley seemed to have my back on this.

No, Hank. Only the men folk and then only men like we are. What we are. It's both a gift, and a curse. But I 'spect now you're gonna hear everythin'. I just hope you'll be able to hear it all and cope. But if you don't, well we're here to help you out.

I smiled softly to my mom that I was okay. She patted my shoulder and took a seat herself while the others settled in around the large oblong dining table: Mama on one side of me, Cory on the other, with Riley and Tanner pulling up chairs to sit between them and me if just slightly behind me, sorta like they was guarding me or something.

Yeah, somethin' like that ... Tanner said in my head.

I smirked but let it go as I had bigger fish to fry with whatever was on my mother's mind just now.

After they was all settled in, Mama eyed them curiously, as if she were weighing something amongst them. When she finally spoke, it was when she was sure that no one else had the floor, either physically or in our own heads. Don't know how she could've know'd the other but her hard stare around the room told me more than enough that she did.

"Now, what Cory and I have to say isn't for another soul beyond this room. Am I clear?"

The boys and I looked amongst ourselves, and we sort of nodded.

"I want an answer from each of you, and you can take it as a vow. Because if you break it ..."

She flung her hand straight out to her side with a pointed index finger to the window behind Tanner, Riley and me, and the instant she did it cracked and shattered, blowin' out into the night. Cory lifted her hand in a beckoning motion and the glass flew back into place, like it'd never been touched.

That really got all our attention but quick.

"Now, I am gonna poll the room. Each of you is to raise your right hand and swear that what we talk about here will stay in this room. Y'all can discuss it in your heads all ya like. But it must *never* pass your lips. To do so and it fall on the wrong ears ... It could be the death of my boy. Are we clear?"

They all nodded with much more determination that time. That made me feel a whole lot better. Well, up to the point about it being a danger to me and all, 'cause that part was a bit scary and I was sorta on the fence about knowing what that could be. Cory often said that for some people ignorance was bliss. Yeah, I wasn't so sure about that before, but I just know'd what was gonna come out now was a game changer. Things 'tweren't gonna be the same after.

She took a necklace what was hanging around her neck and pulled it up out of the top of her blouse. It was a very intricate amulet of a silver circle of a tree branch circling around upon itself. There were little leaves and twigs that sprouted from the center stalk of that bent branch. In the middle hung a small vial with some sort of liquid inside. It was sealed shut with a stopper that was completely covered in silver as well. This whole thing dangled from a long black leather strap and sinew braided necklace. The sinew had been colored black so you only took notice of it in the light.

In all my years of living with Mama and Cory, I never did see either of them dealing in the castin' arts. I heard about women what did it up in the Smokies but I had no way of thinking my mama would've been included in their numbers. Cory was another point altogether. She had secrets. I was only coming to realize just how many she carried with her. I marveled inwardly how you can live with people nearly 'round the clock and still never really know'd them t'all. Mama's voice brought me out of my thoughts.

"Now, if you were all bound like you should've been two years ago, this wouldn't have to go down like this. As it is, Cory and I apologize for the way we gotta do this. It is not meant to slight any of you in any way. Remember, this is for Hank's safety. If you love my son like I think you all do, you will endure anything you have to go through tonight.

"Hank?"

"Yessum?" I answered softly, not sure what was going to happen next.

Her gaze was hard and unrelenting. I was hoping at least for a little motherly sympathy but I saw none of it in her eyes. She was all business now.

"Place your hands on the table palms up."

I looked slightly over my shoulder at Riley, who had slipped to the edge of his chair. I could tell his hackles were up. A quick pulse around the room and I knew all of my boys were ready to spring and fight should something go down. But it was Mama and Cory, surely they wouldn't do me no real harm, would they?

Riley nodded just once and I could feel him and Tanner slip into my head, reaching deep inside to make sure they were feeling whatever I was. I could feel the boys tense up, all of them watching Mama and Cory, as if one word from me, one single moment to rattle me in any way and I just know'd blood and bone would be involved. I had to appease them before it all started to go down.

"Boys, just do what Mama says. No matter what, no matter how much I make shake your resolve, you hold still unless I say somethin' to the contrary, hear?" I eyed each of them and I could tell that despite their wanting to tell me to fuck off, they agreed to it nonetheless.

So I slowly put my hands forward on the table, palms up, just as she bade me.

Before anyone could react, Mama and Cory staked my palms to the table by two long silver skewers. The contact of silver on my skin sizzled and a few tendrils of smoke from my burning flesh were drifting slowly upward. I howled in pain. Riley and Tanner lunged for Cory and Mama, who lifted a hand with the effect of slamming each of them into the wall behind me. They both roared with rage struggling against the unseen hand that held them pinned to the wall. The rest of the boys sprang from their seats and growled broadly, each of them vibrating with anger – raging from head to toe. I saw their features change, like shifting in and out of their normal selves and something more animal like, but they was struggling like they were trying to keep it all in check. It was a battle they were losing too.

In that sheer agony of my palms being pierced I realized I needed to take control of it or that blood and bone I was fearing was gonna happen.

"No! NO!" I panted through the pain. "You all stay put! Back, the fuck, down!"

I let a long puff of air out of my lungs; the pain was intense. I could see Mama's and Cory's mouths moving rapidly; like the course of a river those whispers began to swirl around us again. I tried like hell to ignore it and keep my hands perfectly still so as little of my flesh was touching them silver skewered spikes. The blood from the wounds started to move along the table top like they was following a groove in the wooden table top, smoldering with the same smoky tendrils that wafted up from those two long lines of blood flowing to the very end where it squared off and they joined together.

Mama held the amulet aloft in her hand above my palms and the whispers became a bit more frenzied and she let go of it and it just hung there with no help from anyone.

"Mike!" Mama called out to him, making him jump and he growled tersely at her. She seemed to pay it no mind, though she did have to speak louder than usual to be heard over my boys who were still quite angry at being surprised like they was. I had to admit, I was right there with them on this score.

She instructed him to raise his right hand. Mike howled and snarled fiercely at her but held his ground as he watched me with intense eyes that were as red as the blood along the table. The whispers began to move about in a torrent the room. I looked over to Cory and saw that she was speaking softly but there was way too many of them voices to have come from just her and Mama. I didn't know where they were all coming from, but it was just like those what I heard earlier this afternoon when that stuff went down in Mama's room.

A tendril of smoke snaked its way toward Mike's snarling mouth eliciting a new round of growling from him. I could see the fear in his eyes. He was trying like hell not to show it, but as that tendril came into contact with his face, I felt him inwardly shudder. We were connected, the binding stronger than before. I felt him take root in my heart, almost as if the beating of my heart was falling into synch with his. I calmed my breathing as best I could and called to him through my mind.

Mike, hey, Mike. Listen to me. I'm okay. It burns but I am right here, okay?

I could see this had the effect I was going for. His snarls became much more controlled, almost subdued entirely. Mama nodded before moving on. Each in turn was asked to do the same thing, with the last two being Tanner and Riley who were allowed to return to their seats when the circle was complete. The anger in each of them was costing me what little resolve to just hang on to dwindle to almost nothing. I don't know where I found the strength to deal with it all, but the thought of causing my boys any more pain than I was already under took nearly what little energy I was quickly running out of.

By the time the link was complete Mama and Cory retook their seats.

"Swear by all that you hold dear to you that no words about this night shall ever pass your lips or be written down or conveyed in some other manner. It *never* leaves this room! Ever! Are we clear?"

They roared, grumbled but nodded once just the same. Agreement reached, however tentative it may be. Mama seemed to take it as their word. Mama and Cory hastily removed the skewers and my hands snapped back to me like they was made of rubber pulled to the point of breaking. I eyed the two of them as I gingerly rubbed around the wounds in my hands that seemed to be healing already.

Mama watched me closely, "Yes, the healing you all can do is quite remarkable."

Riley reached for me, pulling me around in the chair to face him and gently put the back of my right hand to his lips and ran his tongue along the skin, soothing it in ways I hadn't imagined were possible. When Tanner cleaned me up that first time in the forest it had been an amazing feeling as he leeched away the pain from my wound from when Riley had bit clean through that muscle during our sex together in the woods. This was somewhat different, can't say why but it just was.

He licked the inside of my palm too. He moved from that hand to the other and I stopped him. His eyes narrowed a tiny bit wondering what was going on in my head now. I wished him luck with that because I wasn't so sure I knew what I was doing anyhow. But it just seemed right, like I needed to have something to remember this agreement between us all. That sorta stuck in my craw for some reason, like if I didn't carry something from this then I wasn't making the same sorta commitment or something. Yeah, something like that.

I watched the wound slowly, painfully close and heal. The scar that was forming was far more prominent than the smaller, less noticeable one Riley had sorted for me. I brought my hand up as I turned to face them all.

"I don't know what's all going on. I can't begin to imagine what my ma and Cory got to say on it all. And what with the castin' goin' on," I eyed the both of them rather pointedly. Neither of them seemed to flinch much under that, not that I expected it much. I mean, it was my mother and Cory, two of the strongest women I ever did know. But there was something else in the way they were looking at me, something in their eyes that sort of rattled me a bit. I wasn't so sure I wanted to know what they were thinking. It sorta looked like they were proud or something. I quickly looked back to my boys, to something far more comfortable, something I understood.

"But what I do know is," I held up my left hand as the final part of the wound began to close, leaving a rough edged scar after, "I have to bear this mark for what the promise you all made to me. I can't just come out of it," I spared a look at Tanner and Riley, who only smiled a tiny bit at my words, "and have nothing to mark its passing. So I will wear this with pride, pride in what you all have come to mean to me. Now I don't fully know what that means ..."

"But you've figured it out some," Spike shot back with a pointed look from under his brow. The boys all chuckled and I swear I spied Mama and Cory blushed the tiniest bit, and for that I shot Spike a warning look that said he best keep that to himself if he knew what was good for him.

"Yeah, well, even then. But I just want you all to know, I ain't takin' it in vain. I am beginnin' to see how deep this goes. I feel ya all inside me." I touched my heart with my left hand. When I did I felt each and every one of them caress me inside. Each of my boys, they reached out and I felt them. I gasped a tiny bit at how overwhelming that feeling was just then. My boys were powerful strong, that was for sure.

"And I want a reminder of what price you've all paid just bein' here. It means ..." I lost my voice, emotion rushing in like a wave to where I thought I'd start to bawl like a newborn baby. That was something I so didn't want to do. Each of my boys looked at me with such pride that it broke my heart into eight pieces – one for each of them – with precious little left for myself.

I felt a hand on my shoulder from Riley.

"We all know what it means, Hank. You ain't gotta say." He placed a hand on my chest. "We know, in here."

My eyes got all watery with how he spoke and the way he was looking at me, and for a moment, for just that one moment, it was like I was alone with them all. Everything, the world, the store, it all faded away and it was just me, just me and Riley, just me and Tanner, just me and my eight boyfriends.

As if Mama could hear what was inside my head, even if Riley said she couldn't, her next words made me realize just how much she was entrenched in this whole thing. But her words weren't for me, they was for Riley, for the boys.

"It's okay, Riley. I ain't been around Hank's daddy long enough to not know how you boys are around one another. Didn't make my life any easier with the knowin' what with takin' a back seat to it all."

She sighed quite heavily. I could tell that there was a heap of history in that sigh, and somewhere deep inside was the man who helped bring me into this world with her. Somehow I knew she wasn't just talking about me and my boys. She was also talking about my daddy. Somehow she knew what we were all about and how our lives really worked.

Riley just seemed to know what Mama meant by it all and he leaned forward and left the softest and most delicate kiss on my lips, in front of them all. While part of me was shocked by it I realized that this was exactly what Mama was talking about: we boys sticking this close to each other.

"But I get it. It's just the way it is. In a very real way I bear as much responsibility for it as any other woman in this life we have, such as it is." She smiled warmly at Riley and placed a delicate hand upon his strong bicep. "All I ask is that you hold true to your pledge to me, and to my boy that you just took right now, here in this room. Now I know he hasn't turned. I know that he doesn't really know the meaning of it all. And, well, that's what Cory and I are here to tell you, Hank."

She looked to the rest of them in the room.

"To tell you all. It's time you all knew the full history of what has come before, what parts Cory and I played in it. And most importantly, Hank, what part your daddy has played in it all. Your daddy has the biggest role in it. It's also why you are cursed with what path you have before you. You boys need to know it all. Cory and I have decided now is the time to come clean, the only way you boys will survive what's to come is if you have the knowledge of where things are, and sadly, what's ahead for us all."

CHAPTER FIVE

The Maiden, the Witch and the Wolf

"Roanoke," was all she said at first, waiting to see if we had anything to take from that single word.

Now, I know we had that as a history assignment in our first year at Cavanagh so it wasn't too far of a stretch into my past to find out where she was going with it all. That English settlement that landed on the outer banks of North Carolina, only to mysteriously disappear from the face of the Earth three years later, was one of the first mysteries on these here shores. It was a story that was passed down to each generation – shrouded in mystery – with only a single word: *Croatoan*, crudely carved into the post of the settlement as the only clue to the missing settlers fate. But Mama spelled out what she knew of the tale and it varied widely from the one we had been told in school.

"The Roanoke Colony of 1585 was where it all began. Well, began here in the States, that is."

Again she watched us, her eagle-like gaze taking in each boy's face, the subtleties and small movements or gestures in them that might give her a clue on what each of us was thinking.

Only I don't think Mama understood how well we truly were connected. Her little binding spell seemed to do us a whole heap of good on that front alone. I found I could push along that line between us with greater ease now, like them party lines we got here in the store that everyone used at one time or another. Well, it seemed I had my own little party line going on now with my boys. Far more resilient and far more stable.

As my mama and Cory started to tell us the tale of how we all came to be, I would send a small thought or emotion back amongst them all and slowly watch it take root and blossom on their faces as if they thought it all on their own. It was quite the sight to behold. Me and my boys were truly one. I could influence them and they didn't even know it was happening.

A hand on my thigh by way of Riley squeezed just gentle enough to let me know that not everyone was so bamboozled by my little game.

Damn him.

This brought out a smirk to his face that caught me by surprise and I found myself staring at him like he was the sexiest thing I ever did see. Then he flushed a bit but tried like hell to cover it up by scratching his head.

"... And some boys had better pay attention and stop with their flirting 'cause they're in a whole heap of trouble as it is," Mama just turned her head to me with such a pointed look that it caused the other boys to chuckle a bit 'til she rounded on them as well. It was like we was all being in school and getting caught by the teacher.

"This ain't school, ya know. I don't have to tell y'all any of this."

Her eyes were like needles, as if she was the embodiment of Miss Jayne English, who really was our English teacher at school – and had the unfortunate luck in life to have a name that described what she ended up doing in life. Well, that was a reminding that none of us boys wanted to think about just then. If anything was gonna put us *out of the mood* it was anything having to do with Miss English. She was about as sour a woman as you *never* did wanna meet.

"Yessum," I said sheepishly while the other boys sorta smirked and tried their best to hide it. My eyes glanced at Cory who was struggling to keep her face as straight and plain as Mama wanted us to be about such a serious a subject as who and what we was. Then I got to thinking what the hell was I doing that caused all of this in the first place – *oh yeah, I had me eight boyfriends who I needed tendin' to all their lovin' needs.*

Just that thought alone had a couple of them squirming in their seats.

"That's better, Hank. And I'd suspect that you, more than any of the others at this table should be payin' attention to this whole thing as it concerns you most of all, son! You and your daddy are too much alike, thinkin' with your other head too damned much."

"Mama!" I nearly yelped in absolute shock that she'd say such a thing, let alone admit that Daddy was the same damned way – and with *boys,* no less.

Who'd you think did the turnin'?

That thought snaked into my head but I didn't know who it belonged to. My eyes quickly scanned the room but none of them was willing to look right at me. It was bewildering, too much to process in my head that Daddy, that big mountain of a man, a man's man as Mama'd like to say so often about him, that he'd ever touch another boy like I had.

Oh, he did far more than just touched ...

Again, that voice – dark and heavy but clearly none of my boys from what I could tell, unless he was extremely good at hiding who he was, which didn't seem likely. No, this voice in my head was decidedly different. And *he* seemed hell-bent on keeping himself hidden from me. For now, at any rate. Why I could say that, I didn't rightly know. But it was just a lingering caress across my mind that he wanted me to know that he wasn't going to stay hidden long. I didn't know why this was so, but it was very clear that he wanted me to know this aspect of his presence. And it seemed that, as I looked about my boys, that it was meant solely for me.

"Don't you Mama me, boy! It isn't as if I don't know that part of your lives. Your daddy had more than his share of being *out with the boys*."

Her gaze softened just a bit before she continued.

"The life you will lead, the lives we all are leading in this hellish part of the mountains, is not an easy life."

Her gaze wandered off somewhere else now, somewhere that had little to do with me or the world I had grown up in. She was somewhere far off, a world that she alone seemed to know about, something separate from us.

Apart.

"But that'll come soon enough, I should think," she continued.

Her gaze refocused itself on those of us in the room, just as pointed and driven as it had been when she first arrived in the store a few minutes before.

"Mama?"

She looked at me with no small amount of concern floating there across her eyes. She was still my mother after all. That had to account for something, didn't it?

"Yes, baby," she said as she ran a gentle hand along my own on the table top.

I blushed a bit at her being so motherly around my boys, but it seemed they didn't mind so much. Actually, they sort of seemed warmed to the idea that this store, our lives, were now part of theirs, like my boys had a place to call home.

You are our home ... Riley caressed my thoughts with his own. *Wherever you are, that's where we'll be. All of us.*

I nodded once to him; he smiled, as did the others. We were of like mind, a pack, one.

She was still waiting for my reply.

"What exactly *are* we?"

Eyes met eyes, gazes locked then moved on. I wondered just who was going to answer me honestly? That's what I wanted; that's what I craved. Hungry for it, I was. Nothing short of it would satisfy. They all seemed to know this. They all had something to gain or lose with their next words. Gaining my sanity in all of this didn't mean that they'd have to give up much, did it?

I wondered ... what could be so damning? What could be so disastrous that my simple knowing would bring the walls tumbling down around us?

Silence.

Deafening, brutal silence met my query.

There was a flash, brief but powerfully felt, that I hated them, hated them all for their smugness that their knowing something I didn't or was thought couldn't know, as if I was to be coddled, protected from myself, protected from knowledge of something all too frightening.

"Babe," Riley tried. I stopped him cold.

"No, Ry," my gaze moved to his and I knew my regard for him was pointed; I wanted it to be so. I wanted them all to feel my angst over this.

"You don't get to go there until I have some truth. I WANT ANSWERS! I WANT SOME HONESTY HERE! I don't think that this is an absurd thing to request. You all need to stop mollycoddling me and give me some straight up answers. If'n I am in the middle of this here situation, then by God, I need me some god damned answers – and NOW!"

I was huffing by the end of it; the tip of my finger was a bit sore from how much I was pounding it upon the table during my little speech.

"Hank, your language," she began but I cut her off too.

"No, Mama! I will not, no ma'am, not for one god damned minute, do you understand me? I am a man and as such I demand respect and honesty in this here house. I am my *father's* son! You keep sayin' I am so like my father," I was shaking my head emphatically at this point. I didn't care. They all said I was in the middle, that I was their so-called leader in this, then by God, I was gonna get in the middle and start leading.

"Well, let's get to the meat of the matter, shall we? I am letting you all know," I said pointing that sore finger at them, all the fury in my face making me shake all over, "no more! I swear it: no more lies, no more keeping shit back! No more half-truths! Y'all git me?"

I huffed, repeatedly. No one knew what to do. I could see it plain on their faces.

Fear – as if I'd just become something monstrous.

"Do you?" I bellowed, my voice so powerful that several panes of glass cracked and the table rumbled from it all. A low hum permeated the entire building before it too slithered away.

I slowly turned my head at an angle, as if I was trying to work out a kink in my neck. I heard something snap inside, something akin to a knuckle crack, or a joint popping back into place.

No one moved.

Finally ...

"As you say, my son," Mama said softly, but resolute in how she had handed over the reins on our lives to me. I could feel it. I could tell that somehow I had crossed a line I could never return from.

But she wasn't quite done, it seems. She raised a brow, and had that look upon her face whenever she had decided I'd learn in my own good time whatever foolishness had crept in and taken root, as if life itself would be my final arbiter. For a moment, I worried.

For a moment, I knew true fear.

But my mother had motherly concern and love for me. I didn't allow myself the folly of thinking that life had any such affection for me. It just wasn't in the cards for the likes of me. I knew that; I wasn't that special.

Riley growled darkly. I didn't respond; in this I found my best mechanism to keeping him at bay. Reticence on my part, however small was something that confused Riley. I'd have to remember that. Not that I was planning on deceiving any of my boys. But knowledge in and of itself, no matter how I came by it, was to be tucked away and kept close to the heart.

"So, Roanoke," class had resumed, it seemed, "and when I say that I don't mean that fair city to the east of us. I mean it in its rawest and most historical sense. I speak of that doomed *lost* colony."

The way she emphasized that word *lost* implied a helluva lot more than what I expected, as if *lost* didn't mean anything of the sort. But how can Mama, as learned as she is, know more than what historians haven't been able to piece together with any real definitive declaration of the events that unfolded lo' those many years ago?

I didn't know how that could be.

Unless ... I pondered this ... she was a *descendant* from those fated people from our collective past and by extension, to me.

That made my blood run cold. Something that was so deeply entrenched in our past was clawing its way back to me, scraping its way from the darkest part of history; like a putrid and vile hand, mired in something so horrific that it simply wouldn't let go, was reaching out for me now, was threatening my world and those I'd come to love in it. And somehow, the hardest part of it all was that Daddy was involved in all of this too.

That flew in the face of everything I'd ever known about him. Now, admittedly, that ain't saying a whole helluva lot 'cause he wasn't around shortly after my fifth birthday. Yet, if I thought about it, there were signs that had existed even since then, signs I didn't know what to make of at the time, but 'twere present nonetheless.

"Sonny boy, you just keep watchin' the line for signs of a bite, 'k?"

I turned slightly to look behind me at the man who'd come upon us along the creek we was fishin' in. He was a big mountain of a guy like my daddy. I never met the man he was talkin' to, but it was pretty clear they knew each other, 'cause the other man was standin' so close to him they had to be the best of friends. I looked back at the fishin' line to see if there was a tug upon it. No such luck. I walked up to the water's edge and picked up a couple of small stones to try skippin' them across the water like my daddy show'd me. I wasn't havin' much success.

I began to hear Daddy and this man talk in very hard but hushed tones, like I wasn't supposed to hear it, yet somehow, despite my being a bit far from them I found if I turned my head in just the right way I could hear them. I never said it to either of my parents that I could do this; it was sort of a secret I kept to myself. It allowed me to understand my world – hearing those conversations that I wasn't supposed to be a part of. Sometimes all they did was confuse me until whatever it was happened and then it all became clearer to me. Well, at least the confusion sort of lifted a bit that I didn't feel quite so stupid. I could make a little bit of sense out of most of the confusion with the adults in my life.

But this ... this was something I didn't understand. Never would.

Until now ...

So I cocked my head, turning it just that way that would allow me entrance into their world, a world of strange phrases and odd feelings.

"Cal, you ain't been by lately. You missed the last hunt, and 'twasn't one of the lesser ones neither. You know what was supposed to go down then. Randall wasn't pleased by it none. The guys have been restless. They ain't been right ..."

"Don'tcha think I know that? Don'tcha think I feel awful 'bout how it went down? But Ruth had taken ill; we have my son to consider. I couldn't leave him – he's only five for Chrissake!"

"So, get someone to tend to her and your boy. The men need you; it's our way. You know this; you know how it works, Cal. They's restless, for fuck sake. They need you, your body, what you have inside that we hunger for. Goddamn it is like you're some kinda drug and we all can't fight it. We're losin' it, Cal. Really fucking losin' it. Randy most of all. Cora is beside herself with how off the rails he's gotten. Do you know there was that body they found outside of Forks Junction that they don't know who it was? Or even what sex it was? The body was so badly mutilated and torn up it was hard to determine what or who it was. No ID; nothing to identify it."

"So? What's that got to do with us? People go missin' all the time. Shit, there was that man what they found up in the Smokies that 'twasn't from around here. Didn't they figure out he just fell off the mountainside and broke his own damned neck? This was prolly the same damned thing only the bears and such got to them, thassall."

"No Cal, 'tain't what happened. That man? The one you just been goin' about? Yeah, well, if you remember right, that was just after the last time you couldn't be there with the guys, the night your boy was born in Beckley, 'member?"

"So? How do ya figure I had anything to do with any of this? Just seems like a stretch ta me."

"No, it ain't, Cal."

"Yeah? How ya figure it, then?"

"Easy, on account of Cora sayin' that same night you was not runnin' with us was the same night that Randy went missin' for like four days. Same as this last time. Cora thinks ..."

He paused, and I could just feel the hackles of my dad goin' up. The whole thing became a whole lot more hushed. I had to really strain to hear them both.

"Cora, Cora, Cora – you'd think she had some sorta way to track us all from the way you're goin' on."

"She's a witch ain't she? Same as your ..."

"Shhh, dammit, the boy might hear."

That changed things up. I could hear the man pull daddy a bit further away from me, but not so much that I still couldn't hear what they's sayin' to one another.

"Well, all I'm sayin' is that Randy ain't been right lately. And we all coulda used you there like you was supposed to be."

Then I heard a strange noise. It was wet, and I could feel the air change around me, a scent broke across the area – it smelled strong – like my daddy when he got all sweaty from workin' in the store or around the property. Then that was followed by some stranger sounds. I tried to see what they was doin' but the man had pulled daddy around the side of a large oak tree.

"Cal, we need ya, man. We ain't been right for a while now. And I know you need us somethin' fierce. Just to taste ya, to smell ya, to feel ya. Christ, God, I could do ya right here over and over, and I know you want it. You keep givin' off them signals that you need us too. You're starved for it. I can *tell. Don't deny it!"*

"I ain't, I swear." Some more of them soft wet sounds that kept me guessin' what this man, this nice lookin' but big man wanted with my daddy. What they meant to each other 'cause it was clear that they knew each other very well.

"Only, I got my boy here, I need to figure out somethin'. Give me a day or two."

"Can't be more than a day, Cal. The moon and all. We're cuttin' close as it is. You know that. Christ, it's eating you up. I can feel the burn in your belly. You are weak from not bein' with us. You can't deny what you are, what's supposed to be. This is bigger than us. All of us. We're just players in this here game. We ain't the game itself, ya know."

As I slowly came to where they were standin' so close together like Mama and Daddy did back home, that I was confused by it.

"He's comin'. Go, go on an' git."

Another wet sound, a grunt from Daddy, and I heard footsteps slowly retreatin' away from us just as I turned the tree and found my Daddy leanin' his big arm on a branch, watchin' the direction the man had gone off to. He turned to find me there, a smile as warm as the day lit up his face.

"Heya, Hank. How's my boy?"

His eyes glistening as he took me in, scoopin' me up in his big arms and nuzzlin' into my neck for all his worth, makin' my mind go all fuzzy and full with him, the smell of him, the strength in him. He was my daddy; he was the man I loved above all others.

"Still do ..." I whispered to myself as that distant memory slithered away from me.

The lingering scent of my father played back in my mind so clearly that I swore I could smell him now. I've never missed someone so much as

I did my father. It was a hole what's never been filled. Not by my Ma, not by Cory and not even by my boys.

I'd give anything to be in his arms right now, to let him pull me close and say I was his, of him, by him and belonging to no one but him. I needed him something fierce just about now. I was floundering, like a leaf on the surface of a river. I needed to stop and take root, grab life by the reins like he did and start to set my own course.

"Roanoke is something you all have learned in school, right? The lost colony?"

The boys and I nodded.

"Yessum," I replied genial enough that she pressed on with her story.

"Well, from what has been handed down from that time to where we are today, those people didn't just disappear like they all thought had happened at first. Well, least not by some mysterious set of circumstances. They were only a mystery because no one wanted to say what was really left behind with that colony of men and women and children: a man, a very dangerous man, one who came strictly from the old European tales of the forest. A man what walks like a man in the day but by wolf at night."

"Wait a minute; wait a minute. Hold on!" I cried out. This was crazy talk, this was, like our lives was some kinda Lon Cheney Junior horror movie or something come to life.

"So you're all tellin' me that, what? Like I am some sort of wolf man?" I laughed, only I noticed 'twasn't anyone laughing right along with me.

Not good ...

"You've gotta be jokin' here. You're puttin' me on."

No one moved or said a word.

A guilty chuckle bubbled up from my belly, across my lips and was out before I could put a rational thought to it.

I got up so fast Daddy's chair went sailing back and hit the wall behind it, startling them all. I started to pace. I felt restless all of a sudden, like a fire just got lit and I needed to go, I needed to get out. Yeah, to run. I needed to expend some energy.

But I could see my boys starting to stir. They were getting restless all of a sudden and I knew it was 'cause they could feel me coming across that link we shared. Problem was, if I closed it down, if I cut them off, I was really gonna start a panic. I could already tell my boys fed off of me. If I cut them off, they'd fuckin' flip a lid. I know'd they would. It was plain on their faces how much they were watching my every move now.

With my next pass toward Riley, he stood up and tried to grab my hands into his. I shook out of them.

"Uh uh, Ry ... not now. I need to think."

Only problem was all I had was this noise in my head — images of things I didn't understand, things what were said about me, about who and what we were that were out there for the plucking — except the last time I tried to listen in on them Ry had beat me to it and the boys knocked themselves under. I didn't know if Ry would do that again. As I pulled away from Ry, Tanner got up and blocked me from the other side. I didn't think I'd be so successful shaking him off. So I just stood there, facing Tanner huffing out my nose as I chewed mindlessly on a thumbnail – it was a nervous tick I had that I wished I didn't do but old habits and all that shit.

Ry came up behind me and slipped his hands around my hips and set his chin gently on my shoulder. Part of me was a bit freaked out on how Mama and Cory might take all this boy-loving going on but a glance at Cory told me that they sorta expected shit like this now. Honestly, the whole thing made a heap of sense in answering questions I'd always had about why Cory was here with us and the little odd things that would come out in our conversations, things that seemed on the surface to be simple little inquiries into my day. Only now with what I'd just been given, I can see as plainly as the nose on my face that she was really fishing for where I was in it all.

Tanner pulled me to him with Ry along my backside. 'Twere like we was a man-meat sandwich or something. I just laid my head on Tanner's broad chest and listened to his heart for a few. It was a comforting sound.

"You okay?" Ry asked softly in my ear.

I nodded. I mean, I wasn't okay. I wasn't okay with a whole lot of what was going on but hey, I needed to hear all of it so if I feigned it a bit, I just might get the whole gist of it, *then* I could decided if I was *okay* with any of it. Right now, the jury was still out.

That seemed to satisfy them, either because they realized that I wasn't okay but was calm enough to let Mama and Cory continue or because I'd successfully kept that part of the whole equation out of the mix from them. Either way, they allowed me to retake my chair from the wall and pull it back up to the table. I decided to make light of the situation.

"So, I'm the real Lon Cheney, Jr., then? Is that what you're sayin'?" I asked Mama and Cory. It was Cory who answered.

"Not anything like that Hollywood mumbo-jumbo, Hank. Believe me, it's a whole heap of a bigger mess than the simple filmin' they do in them movies. My Randall used to complain all the time about the change. He said the transition is something quite painful. Didn't much like it. Was okay once he took his lupine form, but the crossin' over was *a real bitch*, as he used to say."

She blushed nine shades of red 'cause Cory hardly ever said a blue word in her life. Well, she did, only it was usually only whenever I was around to hear it.

I glanced at Mama and she sorta smirked at Cory being so straightforward about her husband.

"And what did happen to your husband, Cory?"

She turned and looked at me with the warmest expression. What she said sucked whatever life I had flowing in me. "Why, your daddy killed him."

That was the sucker punch of the century! I felt myself inwardly cringe from it. My daddy, a *murderer?*

"No, Hank. *Not* a murderer ..." Riley corrected my wayward thoughts.

"Land sakes, child, 'twasn't nothin' like that. I asked your daddy to kill him for me. For us all, really. Mercy killin' it was, too. Only, well, it caused a heap of strife in the pack because of it."

She studied me for a moment, wondering if I'd taken leave of my senses yet. Little did she know that I thought that little choo-choo had truly gone 'round the bend this time but had left for destinations unknown. All of it was absurd. I thought they all were a bit mad, to be honest. Yet, there was a part of me that said it all fit. Somehow the absurdity I felt wasn't really that absurd at all.

Funny how mysteries that have finally been answered can only leave you more disturbed than the not-knowing in the first place. And in a real way, that was the toughest part of it all, that somehow I'd sorta figured out something about it, only just not to the extent that they all had. Well, I guess they was all in the thick of it while stupid ol' me just wandered around in my own little world, shuffling back and forth between the store and school, just another lonely boy with not a clue in the world what was moving about without him.

"How?"

"Well, hmmm, how should I put this?" She pondered that for a moment. "Let's just say that in your wolf form you boys retain a bit of who ya are in your human life. It's just ... fragmented. Am I right about that boys?"

She looked around and they all sort of shrugged and nodded that her way of saying it summed it up for them as well.

"Well, that's how your daddy described to me anyhow. Said it was like you was there, but inside – could talk a bit along your shared link but it was like a bad party line. Fragments was the word he'd use, pieces of thoughts and ideas. Well, unless something was felt strongly by the whole pack then y'all seemed to be right on the money and the signal is stronger."

"Yeah, Hank," Riley chimed in. "It's how we know when you think them thoughts what gets us all riled up."

"What thoughts?" Mama asked us both.

"Nothin' Mama, just me bein' stupid I guess."

"Hank!" Riley barked and the boys growled darkly, even made me jump a bit when they did that.

"I know. I know, sorry! My trap just gets ahead of me and shit just spills out. I didn't have anybody to talk to like this before. My world was sorta lonely then ... well, before all of this." I indicated to the rest of them before I slapped my elbows on the table and face-planted my head in my hands with my fingers curling into my hair.

I felt a soothing hand along my back, a gentle caress, caring and comforting if a bit odd cause Mama and Cory were still in the room and I didn't think I'd ever get over that odd feeling. I felt the need to explain their behavior to them.

"The boys get all up in arms whenever I think or say somethin' about myself that they don't agree with."

Cory waved a dismissive hand at me.

"Lawd, it ain't like I haven't seen or known what you boys get up to.

My Randall was just that – randy. Whether it was with me or the boys he ran with, it's just how it was. He was an excellent lover, but I knew where my place was in it all. There's something you boys have between you that we, as women, can never be a part of. Don't mean he didn't love me any less 'cause of it. Just different, I suppose. It was the same with your Mama, I 'spect."

I looked at Mama who had a pained and puzzled expression. Clearly she felt the same but there was a fair degree of resentment in their place in it all. I began to understand and feel some compassion for their situation. It couldn't have been easy, no matter how you cut it.

"I'm sorry about that, Mama. Can't have been easy for ya. I mean, you and Daddy seemed fine enough. There were problems. I know 'cause I heard them, even if I didn't really understand them at the time."

She reached out and took my hand again.

"Yes, there was some tension there. But I loved your daddy. Still do. He's a mountain of a man with a backbone in him that I came to admire and clung to greatly. And he loved us."

She wiped a lone tear what strayed from her eyes before she could bite it back.

"Well, loved you more than anything. You're what bound us together, Hank. You are the greatest thing we ever did, your daddy and me. And he'd be so proud of you now. You're just as kind and as thoughtful as your daddy was, and just as handsome – well, you are a bit prettier than your daddy was. He said it came from me – the prettiness about you. He always told me that what we created in you was his most joyful thing in his life. He was so proud of you, Hank. You were life to him. He'd often just stop and watch you play, watch whatever caught your eye. I 'spect he woulda dropped everything in this world, me included, if he could've just taken you away to live with him in the forest.

He just adored you. Even with all the love your daddy had for me, which was plenty abundant I can tell you, even I couldn't hold a candle to you. You were so loved by him."

I couldn't stop the tears from her words. They just flowed silently. This was something I'd always clung to, that remembrance I had of him, of how I'd spy him watching me. How he'd snuggle up to me. Or how he'd just call me to him at night and I'd climb up the length of him and snuggle into his big furry chest and listen to that heartbeat of his – that massively powerful machine inside. I swore I could hear the love he had for me pumping in there. And he'd let me go to sleep there for hours; it'd be just him and me. Eventually, I'd feel him pick me up gently and he'd carry me back to my bed and spoon himself around me until I fell back to sleep. When I'd wake it'd be cold as hell in the room 'cause Daddy'd gone back to his own bed. If'n I ever got scared or worried, he'd somehow know it the minute I felt it and he'd be at my side. Not to pacify me or mollycoddle, but just to remind me that he was never far off. He'd wait patiently until I'd slip away again before he'd let me be.

The boys hung their heads down a bit, not wanting to see how Mama's words had affected me so. But I wasn't so foolish to think they didn't feel what I was feeling about it all.

I slowly wiped my eyes as Mama got up from her chair. Riley pulled back a bit and she pulled me up into her arms. At that moment my hard-as-a-rail Mama seemed nothing of the sort. She seemed weak and frail, like she'd been bent to the point of breaking and there just wasn't much more she could give just then. She wept for a few, burying her face into the cleft of my chest. She turned her head to the side so she could hear my heart.

"I swear, when I'm like this, I can hear him too. Like he's just there, inside you. That powerful and manly heart, beatin' so hard it's like it's challenging God to strike. Like he could bear the brunt of that kind of damnation and still carry on. Defiant, your daddy was. And God Almighty, was he ever defiant about anything having to do with you, Hank."

"Then why'd he have to go? Why couldn't he just have stayed away from the war, then?" I whispered to her. She pulled back the tiniest bit to let me see the confusion on her face at my question.

"What'dya mean, Hank? Your daddy didn't ever leave ya. He went to the war and he came back. Decorated and everything."

"No he didn't Mama, he went and then disappeared. We didn't even have anything to bury, remember? Just some pine box what we put up there under his gravestone cause we didn't get anything back."

She chuckled softly, pulling a small hanky she always kept tucked in the sleeve of her flannel shirt. She blew her nose and then eyed me to gauge my response. Her eyes widened when she realized I didn't know anything of the sort in what she was saying.

"Aw, baby, he did go to the war, but he came back. Only, he got sent back abroad to be a part of the clean-up process after the war. It was supposed to be a short-termed thing. Only from what was told to me, which wasn't much, he got caught up with some of the Russians along the eastern part of Berlin and that's when he went missing. I am sorry if I never made that clear to you. Your daddy was a great man, but he was also a very complicated man. I loved him – I still do, but sweetie, just know that I am sure whatever did happen to him his last thoughts were for us, well, for *you*."

I nodded. I couldn't look at any of them just then. The pain of it all was too much to bear. I missed my father something fierce. It festered and boiled inside me like molten lava sometimes, the burn from it only increasing over time. The only peace from it I found was whenever I could swear I smelled him on the wind. It'd be fleeting, almost a wisp of a scent, like a memory that had lingered there until I happened upon it. Only when I thought I smelled him did I know any peace.

"I'm sorry Mama. I didn't know how hard it was for you and all," I whispered.

This was so personal and here we were just yammering on about it in front of them all. I felt like this sorta talk should be just between Mama and me. Cory seemed to know what I was thinking before I said anything about it.

"Child, it's hard dealin' with the pain of losin' someone. Sometimes it's a good thing to gather those who mean the most to you so you don't feel so isolated. I *think*," she turned her pointed gaze to the rest of my boys, "that these boys would protect you with their very lives."

They all made sure I felt them fully. So much love radiating back to me from deep inside them. I could feel it well before I looked each one in the eye.

"Them knowin' the most intimate part of your life seems like a small trade off to me if they's willin' to do what they have to to protect you. Don'tcha think?" She asked me.

I contemplated Cory's words. She was right about that. As personal as it was to talk about my daddy like Ma and I was doing, there was a comfort in that my boys would do whatever they had to to keep me up, to keep me going. It occurred to me that their knowing about my world and the more private stuff may come in handy at some point. Maybe they'd all have a real situation where I may be in trouble and their knowing about my past might give them a clue about how to get me outta whatever fix I may find myself in. No, Cory was right about that. I needed to let my boys have unfettered access to everything about me, whether it be inside along that link we all seemed to share, or in me allowing them in.

"You lead a pack life now, Hank. These boys are gonna know you in ways that even I can't know. They are as much family now as our own blood kin." She sighed and shook her head slightly. "Hell, with the way these family lines have been so religiously guarded to keep the wolf population down in these here parts, we're all practically related anyhow."

The boys and Cory sniggered a bit at that, with a few of them nodding their heads in agreement.

"So, uh, how did it all start?"

She smiled softly, no doubt seeing how I was taking the reins firmly in my hands now. She knew me, knew the absolute perseverance I had built inside of me. Once I latched onto something I would hang onto it with a ferocity that would rival a dog with a wayward slipper.

"Well now, that *is* a story worth the tellin' ..."

To hear Mama tell it like it happened was more magical than I can express here. I'd like to quote her as precisely as I can but suffice to say that I am just a piss-poor narrator in that regard. But I'll try ...

It seemed that when those people arrived in what would become Roanoke on the outer banks of North Carolina, they couldn't have arrived at a worse time in history to call some place home. But in reality, that was the least of their troubles.

Turned out that they had themselves a monster in their midst.

A man by the name of Seamus McGhee - a man of Scottish and English descent from the borderlands between those two great countries. The very same as our boy Spike.

This little bit of information made all our ears perk up, though none more than Spike did himself.

Anyhow, it seemed that ol' Seamus was a sea farin' man from way back in his youth. Only on one of his travels it had taken him to Eastern Europe. He had wandered off and got himself tangled up with another man who turned out to be one of y'all. The man took a likin' to Seamus and shortly thereafter he turned the lad into a man like him, one of them werewolves.

Seamus pretty much disappeared off the planet for a time there only to resurface in England upon his thirty-fifth birthday. By this time he had established himself to be an adventurer – tellin' tall tales that it seems 'tweren't all that tall considerin' the life he'd led thus far.

When word came about of a group of people headin' out to the new world, Seamus decided that that would be the perfect place to disappear. But ol' Seamus was a smart man. Smarter than the man what made him too. In his time in Eastern Europe he wooed and subdued a witch to create an amulet that would allow him to control his wolf-like tendencies. It was powerful enough that it could prevent him from havin' to transform into his wolf existence if'n he wanted to. But this wasn't without a cost though. If he chose to not turn in the lunar cycle, when the moon became fullest, he could do so. But it brought about a terrible fever and would deplete him until he could complete the change and go hunting to regain his strength. It was a risk he'd have to take in the long crossin' to the Americas.

The journey across the sea nearly did him in. But he was able to endure the sickness that came over him, convincing others 'tweren't nothing more than sea sickness. Twice he nearly got tossed overboard only to pull on whatever reserves of strength he had to show them that he wasn't a lost cause.

Whatever the case, his strife was monitored by a woman on that same ship. A woman of witchin' means. Her name was Mary Glenn. She had gleaned enough about Seamus just by watchin' him to sort out what he was all about. Turned out that Seamus 'tweren't the only werewolf she had come across. She knew what the signs were.

When they arrived in the new colony Seamus made a remarkable recovery within a couple of days. This, of course, was because he had slipped into the night to hunt. Mary had taken to keepin' an eye on Seamus and his miraculous recovery. For a while things had evened out. Seamus even had taken to bein' quite the asset in the small colony. He was a hard worker and as easy a man you could want to talk to.

Still Mary wasn't appeased by his gentle-like manner. She knew of the beast inside, the one that would tear them all apart if she didn't keep an eye to his ways.

Time went on and things started to get bad for the settlers of Roanoke. Supplies were all but gone; the crops hadn't taken root as was hoped. Things were getting to be rather bleak. It was then that Mary noticed that while everyone seemed to be affected, Seamus seemed relatively steady in mind and body.

When Governor John White returned to England to plead the case for more provisions to keep the colony going, it seemed that Seamus took it as a sign to finally strike.

A week out from John White's departure, he began a systematic turning of a few of the men in the settlement, a turning that Mary herself had witnessed. That night she hatched a plan to ensnare Seamus and those of his kind.

A couple of nights later she wooed him openly, plied him with a bit of drink and drugged him with a poison with hallucinogenic properties to it. She bedded him and began a pseudo-courtship to keep him close to her. Mary was purportedly a very pretty and beguiling woman so she didn't have to work so hard to ensnare Seamus none.

Within a fortnight the gulf between wolf and non-wolf was growin' ever wider. The natives in the area who had attempted relations with the settlers, now were in full retreat or outright hostile to them. The medicine men amongst them seemed to sense or have evidence that something was not right with the colonists.

This was made worse because several natives surrounding the settlement had gone missing. At first the settlers themselves were blamed which only inflamed tensions between them, despite the best efforts of the settlers to convince the native communities of their innocence in the missing Indian villagers.

When a group of Indian children were found murdered outside the settlement the retaliation was swift and exacting. Several settlers were killed in the crossfire between the natives and the werewolves. For you see, those men what had been turned by Seamus struck back, only to be stymied by Mary who seized upon the opportunity she had been waiting for.

Using her magic, she was able to subdue several wolves to where the natives could kill them as any other wolf in the woods. Of course once they died at the hands of the natives the men returned to their normal human selves – terrifying the natives who ran away from the horrors they'd witnessed. The battle only served to drive the remaining colonists away from the colony to be lost to time.

Only one lone wolf had survived the melee: Seamus McGhee.

He squared off with Mary.

A battle of blood, bone and muscle versus the power of a lowly, but clever kitchen witch seemed fairly equal, but a quick move by Seamus had left Mary battered and bloody. In the motion Seamus made to kill Mary she saw him exposed and vulnerable and she struck with a force what pushed the wolf back onto a broken tree branch and it pierced the body of the wolf with a fatalistic force.

As Seamus gasped his last breaths, Mary dragged herself up and began a different incantation, one that she hoped would rid the world of these werewolves. However, no matter how clever or lucky Mary had been at this point, the task what she chose to undertake was well beyond her basic means. But cast she did.

Only, she inadvertently released the magical spirit of the wolf into this land. So while Seamus expired and he lost the battle with Mary, he had unwittingly succeeded in winning the war.

You see, ol' Seamus had gotten Mary pregnant and that spirit what she released into the world to rid it of the horrors it brought, sought out a different target, that of her unborn child.

Along with a few other settlers who survived, they disappeared into the landscape taking with them the boy who would continue the line of wolves that we have to this day.

"But Mama, I don't understand how you came to be in the middle of all of this."

"Well, it was in part because while the wolf line can only be the men folk amongst us, the women they became involved with began to see that their sole protection was to become the true descendant of Mary Glenn. So for as long as there have been wolves in these here hills, the women have culled from their mates and educated them in the ways of magic to protect the families that were being created."

I pondered this for a bit. While it all sort of fell into place real neat like, I still had some reservations about it all.

"So only men can be wolves?"

She nodded, though Cory had more to offer.

"And not *every* boy is born into it. For a while your daddy and ma thought you had escaped the curse, only to find out by your fifth birthday that not only were you like your daddy, you were going to be twice the wolf he had become. Amplified, as it were. Bigger, stronger, and wieldin' a power that no wolf has ever seen. And make no mistake, Hank, your daddy was awesomely powerful. Men feared your daddy when he got angry. Even alphas of other packs would take notice if'n something got under your daddy's skin. It didn't make him many friends in the wolf community, I can tell you that."

"But why was daddy so danged powerful? Did that happen naturally?"

"That would be because of me," Mama said softly. "I thought I could cure him from that life. It was a huge risk, but your daddy wanted to be free from it. We found out you were on your way to us and your daddy wanted to be rid of that life so badly that it consumed his every thought. It was dangerous but we had to try. Your daddy said that he didn't want that wolf anywhere near you when you was born. And he had his reasons. Not every father takes to his sons. It happens in nature and if anything, your wolf-like nature can subvert your more human reasoning. It's a danger that every married couple faces in this way o' life."

"But why marry? Why have children at all? Seems to me that the best course would be to simply stop havin' babies and let the line die out."

She frowned a bit, but I could tell in that expression that it wasn't something someone else hadn't said many times over before. I didn't think I was gonna like the answer much.

"Many tried that. But the need to create from the wolf's standpoint is too great. It's in the wolf's nature to ensure the line. So even if the man involved has made a conscious decision to not have sex with women, be she a girlfriend, wife or whatever, his wolf nature would take that choice away from him. Sometimes it could come in the form of outright rape if that is what was necessary for the line to continue. Nature is a very powerful thing, Hank. A human can reason it out; a wolf knows only to ensure that they continue. That's a very big thing to push back against."

She was silent for a few, her eyes darting to the boys in the room.

"It'll be the same for all of you, I suppose, at some point in your lives. The need to carry forward will become too great to ignore. The drive to seed the next generation will outweigh whatever conscious decision you might have to end the line. In the end the wolf always wins. It's why they have endured throughout time as it is."

We were all silent for a spell after those words, each of us taking it in. I could already feel rumblings inside of each of them pushing back against the idea of marriage and children. We were young. Sex was on our minds, of that I was convinced. I had been party to it enough now to know my boys and their need to seed. It was the long-term responsibilities of marriage and family that was not so warmly received.

"What did you do that made things the way they are? With Daddy and all."

She sighed, looked at Cory squarely until there was some sort of unspoken agreement between them before she answered me fully.

"Like I said before, I tried like hell to rid him of the curse. The only problem was that, like Mary, I wasn't strong enough to pull it off. I don't know if any woman is, knowin' what I know now."

"And this made him more of what he was before?"

She nodded, and I could see a fair amount of pain in that simple reply.

"Your daddy was an awesome sight to behold in wolf form. Nearly double the other men in the packs. Alphas bowed to your father, Hank," Cory said quietly, her gaze somewhere far off as if she could see it all before her again.

"What happened to your husband that you asked my daddy to kill him? If you don't mind my askin' though I hate to bring up something that you wouldn't want to think about."

She patted my hand gently.

"Child, I ain't ever held nothin' back from you when you asked me in earnest. I ain't fixin' to start now, neither."

She glanced at the boys, then back to me. It was then that I realized that they still knew something that I didn't and they were both keeping it from me.

"You see, it sort of has something to do with what your mama and daddy tried to do to get him to not be who he was." She shot a glance directly at my mama that I knew was some sort of continuation of a conversation they'd had without me around.

"And just as a matter of record, I don't believe that any amount of power or wherewithal woulda mattered in the least in trying to reverse the *curse* you all seem to think he's under. He was a natural born wolf, Ruth. Now if he was turned, if he wasn't born to the life I think you may have had a real shot."

Then to me, "As it was, I think what they tried to do only rebounded and like when Mary Glenn tried to undo the curse altogether and it rebounded on Seamus' unborn child, the same happened to you. Only, from what your mama and your daddy shared with me later, it was all too clear that as you was growin' up, you were exhibitin' talents that clearly pointed to your being far more than any wolf we'd ever seen. There's no denyin' it, Ruth. Even Cal had come to realize just how different your boy was, er, is. Sorry, Hank, didn't mean to sound like you weren't around. Seems to me that there's been more than enough of that. Lord, child. There were times I swear I wanted to just grab you and tell you all of this. Times when I just know you was strugglin' with it all," she turned a pointed gaze at them all. "Times when I'd be kickin' these boys' behinds for teasin' ya."

Toby started to open his mouth to protest. Even I knew that was a bad idea when Cory got to going on about something. Silly boy that he is.

"And don'tcha try and tell me it was to see what he was made of, neither Toby Moynahan. You boys was just plain mean about it on account of Hank bein' so damned special and you all couldn't stand it! And you let 'em do it, Riley Raintree. So don't you try to come to Toby's defense. Them here boys git it because you were the one eggin' them on."

She slapped the table with the flat of her hand at that to emphasize her point. I really didn't think she needed to. As it was, the boys shied quite a bit from Cory when she got the bee in her bonnet about something.

I glanced at Riley who just sort of shrugged but at least had the wherewithal to look ashamed about it.

Don't worry, Ry. I still love ya. Though I may have to kick your ass later about it.

He sorta smirked to let me know message received loud and clear.

"And don'tcha be lettin' them off the hook about it, Hank!" she bellowed at me.

"Christ, Cory, are you *sure* you can't read our minds too? Sure seems like ya can. Spooky thing that is ... I'm just sayin'."

"No, I can't but I been around you wolfmen long enough to know how you all think about everything that you think about. And now you've got me all twisted and flustered, dammit. The *point* I am tryin' to make is that what your daddy and mama did, compounded your already difficult situation. But to answer your original question ..."

"Shit, Cory. That was so long ago I forgot what I'd asked." I rolled my eyes at how she could go on and on if I let her. The boys stifled a chuckle from my cheek. Cory just plowed right over that. Bee in her bonnet, indeed.

"You *asked* how'd I got around to askin' your daddy to kill my husband – his alpha, I might add, and yeah, that means somethin' to y'all now, don't it?"

The boys nodded. Their ears perked up; it appeared that no one had spoken to Cory about what my daddy had done back then.

"Well, there was a time before all that came to pass where my Randy just wasn't right. Something happened on one of their hunts. I can't rightly say what it was, neither. But he just 'tweren't right towards the end. On the night your mama took ill with a bad fever, your daddy missed one of the boys' gatherin' and something didn't go right. The boys came back but no Randy. He sorta up and disappeared. Then about four days later he showed up on our back porch naked and bloodied all to hell. I got him inside and cleaned up. He slept for at least a good three days after that. Thankfully I was able to keep things goin' until then. Shortly thereafter we found a ..."

"Body ..." I offered. This fit right in line with that conversation that Daddy had with that mysterious man so long ago.

"Yes," she said softly, as if she had put it together that I knew more of this tale than they all realized.

"I actually heard this part when Daddy and me went fishin' the crick back when I was five, just before he went off to the war. Is that why you asked him to take out your husband, Cory? 'Cause he was killin' people?"

She nodded, a pained expression moved across her face like a cloud eclipsing the sun. I hated that I said it so plainly when it had to have been the hardest thing she had to do.

"Ya see, Hank, there just wasn't any way around that. This goes way back before our time here. The wolves have a strict pact that no human life shall be forfeited lest the whole were population would be discovered. No one wants that sorta scrutiny to come here, what with those camera crews and reporters – well, we West Virginians don't take too kindly to others pokin' in our business. So a long time ago all of the packs that run in West Virginia agreed that any huntin' was for *game* only. It's a hard line to toe on account of your minds bein' so fragmented when you're in your wolf form. And we all quickly discovered that my Randy had crossed that line. And not just once either."

"But why my daddy? Why'd he have to do it?"

"Well, on account of who your daddy was to them. Do you understand, Hank?" Mama said softly.

"No ma'am, I do not. No one has explained that part of it. Daddy is a complete mystery when it comes to that. I don't like the not knowin'."

She seemed resigned to something inside, something that she wanted me to see.

"Give me your hand, Hank."

I started to reach for her but she gave me a look what stopped me cold.

"*Take* my hand, Hank. *Take* it like you want to *take* something from me. I want you to *take* that which you want to know."

Each time she said the word *take* I got a little woozy, as if she was casting something on me. I shook it off, a little perturbed that she'd do such a thing to her own boy. In truth, it sorta pissed me the fuck off. So I did *take* her hand – and hard too.

And I fell ...

The rush was intoxicating. I could hear voices all around me whispering, with some screaming at me in the distance. They swirled around me, black with fury. They were rattling and beating as loud as they could but never quite rising above the din. It was like what I'd imagine being in the middle of one of them cyclones – a flurry of noise all around, so much that it was visible to me, but never so much as to come close enough to give me warrant for concern.

Pull it from me, Hank.

Her voice was so soft, like a caress along my ear. Somehow it cut through the raging voices as if they weren't a problem at all.

Find what you want to know and pull it!

I realized she was guiding me.

So I formed the question in my head:

Show me what happened to my daddy the night it all changed.

The room shuddered 'til I thought the ragin' cyclone was gonna tear everything apart. Then as if my question was strong enough, the whole thing dissipated in a matter of seconds. I was still sittin' at the table but I was alone now. It was late at night and my mother was gathering a few things from the kitchen area: a couple of candles, some salt and other odd things. I noticed that her belly was slightly protrudin' and I realized that I was watchin' a memory of hers and that little bump was me.

"Are ya all ready down there?" she called out.

From the basement I could hear my father's voice, "Yeah, I feel plumb crazy doin' it but yeah, it's done."

She had a small smirk playin' across her lips though it didn't quite reach her eyes. Her eyes said that this was nothin' but serious.

She scooped up the last of the ingredients and started down the stairs to the basement of the building.

The walls around me smeared, the color running as if someone had poured turpentine across my vision only to be cleared away a few disorienting seconds later where I saw her comin' down the stairs to find my daddy layin' back in a big wash tub like he was the heap a-laundry what needed done.

Mama just smirked before a small laugh bubbled outta her as she set her things down. She turned to take him in fully, 'cause there was Daddy in all his masculine glory – and he was truly glorious. I found if I possessed one tenth the amount of manliness he had goin' on then I'd be pretty danged proud of myself.

So there he was, butt-assed naked, in a bath of basil leaves and other herbs, complete with lavender buds and petals, and some herbs I couldn't begin to sort out. All I remembered is that they were on a very high shelf so that Mama had to use the tall ladder to get to them. They were her "special" herbs and I was not to touch them.

"Yeah, yeah, I get that the wolf is in the bath water with flowers. You don't have to make it more awful than it already is."

She laughed softly; finding humor in a serious situation was a sight to see in my parents. I knew they loved each other but their intimate moments were few and far between. It was nice seein' this part of them.

"Yeah, well, I'd kiss you but ..." she tossed a finger towards the bath Daddy was sittin' in, "seein' how we got little junior in the oven I can't come anywhere near that."

"Fucking petals for gods' sake, if the guys ever hear about ..."

"And like I'd tell them? Please Cal, you know that we keep that part of us hidden. None of them know what witchin' ways I get up to around here. Hell, I waited until our second year of marriage before I even told ya what I was."

"I recall ... Don't think I'll rightly be chasin' ya like that again."

She chuckled again as she began to pour a circle of salt around the perimeter of the bathing tub. She was whispering somethin' under her breath, bringing a cascade of whispers along with her that made the salt start to glow real pretty-like. Blue-white, it was.

"What? We startin' already?"

She nodded but continued to cast her spell as she completed the circle. As the circle was completed, she flicked her hand toward the four tall candles, two forest green and two white, that were on column pedestals that took up what I realized were the four points of the world: north, south, east and west — white to the north and south points and the green to the remainin' two. With that wrist flick the candles lit at once, makin' my daddy jump the tiniest bit bringing a deep growl from his belly. She took no notice of how all of this was

*challengin' his inner wolf. I could feel it. I suddenly felt trapped too. I wanted
to get out of there; I wanted to run. But I forced myself to stand my ground.*

*Voices began to murmur along with her, so many of them like bees to a
hive. It made my daddy take notice too; his hackles were up. He became alert
and took to a kneelin' position with his feet cocked to bolt should something go
awry.*

*Her words became more muddled as she came to stand in front of him.
Her arms went out to her sides with her fingers splayed, her head tossed back
with her eyes rolling back to where they was nothin' but whites showin'. It was
very off-puttin'. I didn't like what I was seein'. I wanted to grab Daddy and
run like hell wouldn't have it. Just run and run to get as far away from it all
as I could. Only they didn't see me. I wasn't really here. I had to keep
remindin' myself of that. But it was all so real.*

*Only it wasn't … well, not for me. This was my mom's memory, not my
own.*

*Then I was slammed inside – from her eyes, no longer a bystander but
now I was the willing participant.*

*And I saw what she was trying to do. She was attempting to cleave the
wolf from the man. The words were lost to me; the muttering of them, the
rapidity of how fast they was pourin' outta her was too much for me to even
begin to understand. But I felt what she felt: power, unbridled and wild. She
was pullin' it from the earth itself, like there were rivers and streams of it
coursing around the world and she knew how to access it. It came up through
her bare feet and coursed along her legs into her hips only to start to take root
alongside me in her belly.*

*White light, searing pain engulfed me, followed by bright flashes of green.
The heat was beyond bearable; I wanted to scream, to yell to tell her to stop,
but I was entirely helpless to do so.*

I shook, like being stung by millions of bees. The pain was unending. I knew what she was doin' to my daddy was the same she was doin' to me.

Her head snapped forward again to find my daddy floatin' in the middle of the air above the wash tub, the water and few petals caught on the hairs of his body, his arms slightly outstretched, his head thrown back, his large thick cock was engorged and throbbin' like he would shoot at any moment. His muscles were visibly rippling, alternating 'tween flexin' and relaxin' but in a very unnatural manner. He looked like he was caught between agony and euphoria. His mouth was slack and then taut with a strangled scream. Then he began to transform. The crack of his bone and joints as his body tried to complete the process, only to be stopped and reversed, was deafening. Inside, in my own agony, I felt for my daddy. I wanted to reach out to him so bad that it hurt more than the pain I was endurin'. His back arched, throwin' his head back and he bellowed loud into the air – that strangled roar broke from his lips as if he had punched through solid ice in a frozen lake. The small clerestory windows cracked and few of them shattered.

She began to bellow words that were so foreign in tongue and vehemence that I had no way of repeatin' them if I tried. She spewed them from her mouth, a vomiting of power. I could even feel the spittle from those words as they percolated along her lips. This was a horror beyond anything I could've imagined.

He fell inward upon himself almost to a fetal position, hangin' there in the air. The water would rise up in a column and surround him only to fall back leaving it drippin' off of him landin' in the bath below.

Her words were amplified by the voices that swirled around them, nearly blocking out the rest of the room around them. The vortex began to pull upon them both. Things moved about the basement. Large bags of feed tossed like paper to crash into the walls and dash their contents around the room. Neither of them took notice of the mess they was makin'.

Mama brought her hands in and pressed upon her belly. Inside I felt like

I was bein' squashed into oblivion. I wanted to bellow. I wanted to scream but had no voice with which to do so. A force that felt like it was tearin' me in two pulled upon me; the pain was unbelievable. I shuddered, shakin' violently inside her belly.

I could feel her pull her hands from her stomach and a part of me was being torn. I could feel the violence of it all but with no way to give voice to my pain. A deep, dark snarl emanated from Daddy. He roared into his own chest and shook violently, and somehow I heard him; I heard the anger of that wolf, the anger what was being vested on us both. I could feel him reach out to me. I knew he saw me inside Mama and an anger built up within him. He roiled with it.

One thing was clear, in all of that pain, agony and violence, one thought shattered it all: You shall not harm my son!

Everything seemed to lose all sound, like we all went deaf. Only it had back built until I could feel it coil up, shakin' with a fury all its own. I knew this wasn't Mama no more, this was all Daddy. It felt manly, violent, sheer strength, dominant. The room shuddered with that back build. It coalesced and focused upon him, like he was absorbin' everything she had put out there and was usin' it for his own purposes.

And when he could bear no more, when he nearly succumbed to its power, he broke — he flung himself open from that curled-up position and it threw Mama back some from the sheer forcefulness of his explosive release. His feet came to rest on the ground as if he stepped off of some invisible platform – wolf's feet – upright as if a man, but the wolf had truly emerged.

Not a second later and he was on her. Hand to her throat, he lifted her up so her face could meet his. He snarled. She tried to force him to release her. Nothing worked. He was too strong in this. He pushed her up against one of the posts that held up the floor above. She struggled. I could feel her life ebbing, takin' me with it.

"The ... ba-by, C-a-l ..." she sputtered.

He snarled in her face and then let her go. She sank to the floor, coughing. He stood up tall and bellowed to the ceiling above. Jars shattered on the shelves; more of the stock tumbled to the floor. He kicked the large tub of water and sent it spiraling away from him in a mash of bent metal and liquid. Mama scrambled up from the floor as the water started to reach her. She just made it to the stairs when Daddy moved off into the basement toward the side door. He grabbed the door handle and nearly ripped it from its hinges and he was gone. An ear shatterin' cry cut through the night. Mama sagged to the steps and wept.

Inside though, inside something started to form. Inside her, something from their dark magic had taken root. I felt it as it reached me, the tiny part of them both that was me. It tingled and soothed the pain I had been under. It sorta spoke to me, not in words but in feelin's. And I knew, I knew then that something else had joined with me. Something incredibly dark, something ancient, something binding. Something that I knew I could never truly separate from myself.

A gift from Daddy.

It seemed that Mama wasn't the only witch in these woods now.

CHAPTER SIX

The Witchin' Hour

I let go of Mama's hand in a rush followed by a huge intake of air as if my lungs was deprived of it for a long while. I shook my head a bit to get things moving again and looked up at my boys.

They was all just sitting there staring at me like I was the crazy one.

"What?" I asked them all.

"They don't know what just happened, Hank," Mama said under her breath.

"What do you mean they don't know what just happened?" I asked her without saying it under *my* breath. Seriously, this whole talking out the sides of our mouths was just getting ridiculous and had to stop.

"Well, to them, you only just took my hand then gasped and shook your head. They don't know about the other business."

"But, uh, but, that was like several minutes of stuff that went on there, Mama. Whatcha mean they don't know? And okay, I know they weren't in the whole thing; I ain't that stupid."

"We ne'er said you was," Tanner offered. "You're one of the smartest guys I know."

"Well, then you're in a whole heap a trouble then, 'cause I ain't as smart as all that," I countered.

"You're a helluva lot smarter than you let on, too," Mama said with such defiance that I knew better than to smart-off on that one.

"But the connection thing?" I looked at her, wanting to know for myself what had just happened.

"It's something only you can do. I warned Riley about it, son," Cory offered. "That's why he ordered the boys to close down on your link when he saw what you were about to do. Consider it a gift from your daddy. He had that ability too."

"It hurt like hell, too, when we had to drop off like that," Mike said running a hand along the back of his neck, but he smirked at me so I know he was only ribbing me a bit on it.

"Yeah, okay. I know that was dirty o' me," then to Riley and Tanner, "and you're right. I wouldn't have been ready for it none. Still don't know if I am ready for any of this. But it don't rightly look like I got much of a choice."

"No. Ya don't," Tanner said with a touch more grief in it than I'd like.

"So what'd ya see?" Toby asked softly; his eyes were to the table and he was running a thumbnail along a small groove in the wooden top that I had made many years ago, much to Mama's ire and a solid tanning of my hide. His eyes darted to mine, probably wondering if I was gonna be pissed that he asked. I wasn't. I made sure he saw and knew that. His features softened considerably.

"First off, no secrets. Y'all got that? Not from me. You wanna know somethin', ask whether here," I pointed to my temple and then to my ear, "or here. Either way, you all will have unfettered access to everything that is me."

Mike snorted, "And then some ..."

The boys all struggled to strangle the chortle that came from that small remark. I smiled softly but let it slide.

"And that's for later 'cause while I know it's a part of your lives, I just don't wanna know that," Mama said pointedly. "He's still my boy, even, if he is gettin' up to his manly ways now."

"Aw, Mama ... That's just plain embarrassin'," I rolled my eyes at her.

"I don't care for embarrassing or nothin'. You git me, boy? As your mama, I'm always gonna call it like I sees it, regardless of any embarrassment it might cause you."

"Yessum."

It was silent, the small clock in the kitchen the only sound in the room to mark the time. It was getting late and these boys needed to get on home.

"You never did answer me," Toby pressed again.

"Let's just say that I saw what Mama and Daddy tried to do. And I will tell ya all, but it's way past your supper and bedtimes and Mama will have my hide if'n y'all don't get a move on to your houses. I guess we can meet up early tomorrow at school and I'll tell ya all about it. And that's a promise. Unfettered, and I meant it."

"Okay boys, you heard the man," Riley slapped a hand on my shoulder and looked pointedly at them all. "Best get ourselves goin'. We'll meet at our spot behind the stadium an hour before school."

Like I'd imagine a well-trained military machine, the boys just stood up and nodded their good-byes to Cory and Mama who said their good-nights softly in return. I walked them to the front door of the shop as I heard Mama and Cory move off to sort out something for us to eat before bed.

"I know it's cool outside, but can you leave your window open tonight?" Riley asked me as the boys slipped into the night.

I could feel them mentally slither off in my mind, never so much as to leave me entirely, more to give me some solitude and peace, which I thought was highly considerate of them. They could've just stayed connected in my head and heart and I wouldn't have minded in the least. But it was nice to know that they thought of me anyhow.

"With the way I've been feelin' feverish since that whole bath thing, I don't think I could sleep with it closed now."

"That's the wolf in ya, Hank," Tanner replied, coming up behind me and slipping a possessive hand around my hip and pulling me into his front with no room for second guessing what was on his mind, or Riley's for that matter. They both wanted me again.

Riley smirked, his eyes darting to where Mama and Cory had disappeared to the kitchen to prepare a meal. We were fairly unobserved. Tanner kept leaning down and sniffing behind my right ear and growling while I felt the largeness of him press against me. I began to see why they requested my window remain open.

"Oh," I whispered, well, more like murmured cause Tanner was getting to be aggressive. Riley was right. I knew Tanner would truly test my limits when we'd fuck. I could see bursts of how he'd really like to test me pop into my head, heating my own loins with desire.

Riley took pity on us.

"C'mon big guy, let the man eat. If we're gonna tire him out he at least needs to have a fair chance on buildin' his reserves. He knows what's gonna happen later, he don't need you rubbin' on him through your clothes now."

Riley tugged on Tanner's hand making Tanner moan softly in being so stymied from his lustful ways.

Tanner stopped Riley cold, turned to me and leaned forward, bringing his big hand along the back of my neck and kissed me so deeply that I felt him pull from deep within, making my knees go all weak to where he let go of Riley's hand. He wrapped his arms around me and lifted me off the floor as he drank deeply from my mouth. It was a dizzying feeling, the way he could pull that much from me and I found I only had more to give him. He slowly let me slide down the length of him until my toes touched the floor. His lips parted from mine, though not so far that I couldn't feel their caress as he spoke into my mouth, his eyes searching deeply into my own.

"No, Hank. Never mistake it for lust. That's a part of it, but what you've toyed with in your head is the real thing. We'll be bound to you; not just because it's our way, but we've all fallen in love with you. I know you can feel it."

To prove his point my chest burst with so much emotion I gasped softly, my eyes going wide with how much he was pouring into me. I was flush with him; every part of my body knew the immensity of Tanner Tallman just then.

"Gosh, you are so pretty to look at," his eyes roamed over my face. "I never knew a man could look that way until I spied you a few years back. One minute I was thinkin' other thoughts and then you walked into my line of sight, and everything changed, like a switch was thrown. You ain't ever left my mind since then, Hank. Never will. Now, we may have to marry, we may have to have kids, but *never* doubt that you still hold our hearts and lives in your hands. There's shit we'll have to do, but I am tellin' ya now, all of it will pale when compared to you."

"Yeah, yeah, you big poet." Riley reclaimed Tanner's hand from my waist and began to tug him along. Then to me, he leaned forward and kissed me softly.

"He can go on forever with them big flowery words. You shoulda heard him the first time we made out. He's such a lover boy. He loves being in love. Don't let the big man status fool ya none. He's a big ol' softy when it comes to man love. Night, sexy boy. We'll both see ya later."

"Okay," I murmured to him.

And then they too were gone, slipping away and leaving me some peace. This whole danged thing was upside-down crazy. I ran a mental finger along my heart, like pulling on them trigger lines in a spider's web, each of them cooing back to me letting me know they weren't far off.

I turned to the kitchen as Mama came with some plates for us. It was late and I realized just how hungry I was. Hungry for the life that lay before me, hungry for the men who now occupied it in ways I'd only scarcely imagined but never thought would happen, but mostly hungry for some goddamned food cause it'd been a real long while since I ate!

The curtains on my window billowed softly in the slight breeze we were gifted with that night. Normally I'd've been pretty danged cold but I guess it was what Tanner had said about it, the wolf in me, made my blood run real hot. I was feeling fairly heated all the time now. And when the boys got lustful that heat only escalated to the point where I thought I'd gone completely feverish.

My bedroom was on the opposite side of Mama's and Cory's rooms with the stairwell what let to our upstairs living area running in between them. There was only the one window in my room but it was hinged and swung inside. Before I slipped under the covers without a stitch on, I had opened the window wide to allow Tanner and Riley unfettered access to my room. I smiled softly that my window would probably see quite a bit of action over the years now, and not just from Riley and Tanner. I knew I'd be fairly busy with being with each of my boys now. I didn't rightly know how it was all gonna work but I did have a very real picture that somehow I was the center of it all. My boys were in love with me, and Tanner was right. I couldn't ever mistake it for just plain old lust. There was plenty of that, but this was far deeper. I leaned up against the frame of the window letting the moonlight and night air bathe my naked flesh, sorta smirking that maybe my scent was on the wind to my boys just now, giving them lustful dreams. It was a very lovely feeling.

The Binding.

That phrase was both ominous and awesome to me. I could feel it take root. And it was, rooted. Deeply. It was already bound to my heart and mind in ways that I couldn't even see or feel. It was that immense and strong.

Visions popped in my head of me being coupled with each of them, making love with them, each of them in turn. Then they sorta changed up and it was me with more than one of them, then me writhing with all of them. The effect wasn't lost on my own body as I stood there leaning against the window frame. I smiled contentedly as I pulled myself from the window sill and pulled back the covers of my bed. I stretched broadly before I slipped in and settled in for a light doze before Riley and Tanner'd make their first of what I believed to be nightly ritual. I didn't think my bed would ever be holding just me anymore.

That was a bewildering thought, too.

It was what was in my head as I slipped further from being awake and falling into that warm and deeply loved feeling that was coursing through me as I welcomed sleep.

A musky scent, lingering like a smell I remembered from a long ago memory slithered along my nose. I felt my brows furrow the tiniest bit as I tried to bring myself out of sleep and put a name to that scent. It was vastly familiar and yet totally unfamiliar just the same.

I felt a small pressure along my backside, as I usually slept on my side. I started to move but the feel of a strong man's chest against my back and powerful arm snaked around my waist. His lips nuzzled in on my ear. Hot breath, like a furnace, bathed the side of my face accompanied by a deep, dark growl.

I started to open my eyes when I felt a slick pressure at my ass and knew what was about to happen wasn't right.

Only I wasn't fast enough.

That man. The man whose scent I only barely remembered had forced himself upon me, the thick matte of his chest hair rubbing along my back as he began to fuck me in earnest. I tried to move but then he bit along my neck to keep me in place and I found I couldn't move at all.

Was I was being ...?

Each prod of him, every time he thrust into me was a violation of who and what I was. I didn't know how to fight it. I found I didn't have a voice either. I tried to cry out, and only succeeded in the smallest of whimpers, so soft that I knew it barely was heard beyond the bed let alone the confines of my room.

I started to panic, all the while the man was fucking me slowly, but purposefully, his teeth were painfully erotic as he bit into my flesh. His hands, now fully clawed slowly scraped along my chest and stomach leaving welts along my skin in their wake.

I tried to call out to my boys via our link and found I couldn't find them at all. Whoever this was, he was strong, magically strong, a power that was mirrored in the muscled body he was taking me with.

That's when I realized who this was. That dark chuckle and evil sounding voice from the basement came ringing back to me.

Soon ...

The moment I thought it he practically purred and his fucking became slightly more frenzied. I was powerless against it. Some part of me thought I'd better not fight him. His hold on me, physically and magically, not to mention erotically was working their ways on me.

Some part of me was wailing inside, unable to process that I was a man and I was being raped. Unwanted sex. Sex with no feeling inside binding me to it. Yet somehow, I was able to lock that down. I was able to rationalize how to deal with this. Some part of me that I never knew I had began to strategize how to get out of my situation.

His prodigiously thick and long cock was relentless in violating me.

It was wrong.

I knew it was wrong.

But not because of what he was doing exactly. It was because I was more worried about the consequences.

And then I heard him.

Inside my head.

That dark and possessive voice matched his lust-driven fuck with such heated thoughts that I had to push hard against what he was doing to me. Despite the violating act, he was fucking me to convert me, to bind me to him, magically. That's what was wrong with this. He was trying very hard to claim what wasn't his. That's what I had to push against. A seed of power began to form inside me. But it seemed my attacker had a plan for this as well. Then his voice broke in my head, clouding all thoughts.

Hank you is mine now. Don't bother tryin' to fight this. I'm too strong for you to overcome. You can thank your daddy for that, too. He was my lover for many years and taught me so much. I realize it was what could bring you to me now. Your daddy was just the practice for you comin' into my world. I see that now. Time to claim what's rightfully mine.

He released his hold on my neck and moved my body both with hand and some form of magic I didn't have a clue on how to push back on. He manipulated me into being on my back. He didn't speak a word with his mouth, just in my head. A tiny thread slithered along with his thoughts. It was this voice in my head that had its hold on me and was keepin' me down. Somehow I had to get him out of my head and the spell would be broken.

That's right Hank, I want to watch your face as I claim you. You'll see the possibilities bein' with an Alpha like me can bring. The two of us, together, will be unstoppable.

He pushed my legs apart and mounted me again in one long move, the sensation was mind-splitting and for a moment I gave into his lust. I clutched at his back while some small piece that was crying out for Riley and the boys to rescue me railed in the back of my mind while my body began to respond to this man who was hellbent on possessing me.

Then I recalled who he was, the very same man my daddy had that talk with down by the creek, the man who seemed to know my daddy real well. Those wet sounds from my past now showed themselves for what they were – they was kissing. My daddy was this man's lover. And now he was makin' danged sure I was going to be next.

He began to really fuck me. I gave into it – try as I might inside to find a crack in his magic, try like hell to see his one weakness I could exploit and use against him. But each prodding of his cock was making me weaker in refusing him. That was his ace, where he knew how to undo me. I began to pant with lust for it. My body awakened as if it had a mind of its own, betraying me. I felt more of myself slip away from the sexing my body craved. *It* wanted pleasure from this. A dark chuckle bubbled from the man's lips.

I could feel him back build into his orgasm. I felt it about to burst and claim me for him, taking me away from my boys and the deep love I had for them. I pawed at him, feebly, a strangled cry of pain and agony whispered from my lips. This was how I was going to lose everything. This was how my whole world was going to be taken from me. Not with a real fight but a whimper of regret and pain mingled with a sickening lust.

Just as he was about to cum, a large flash ripped through the room, blinding me, crashing through the roof of the building and pulling my attacker from me and hurling him into the darkening night above. I watched through shielded eyes the look of shock and horror as he flew through the night sky, growing fainter by the moment until he was there no more.

I broke.

A wail loud and filled with anguish broke from my lips, all the hurt and torment coming to the fore. All the pain of my boys being silenced in me cried out for them. Within seconds lying bare and naked, violated and covered in splintered wood and roof, I began to sob uncontrollably, my legs still parted, exposing to the world, that part of me what was for my boys.

Dirty, shamed. I'd lose their love for sure now. So I wailed, spit and anguish pouring out of me. My head thrashed from left to right on the pillow, anger mixed with doubt and fear. A sickening feeling overwhelmed me.

I should've been stronger. I should've been able to resist. But he surprised me. He took me unaware. I was a foolish boy, not a man. I let my guard down, thinking I was growing into my new role with the wolves of my little town.

I put an arm across my face, hiding behind it as the tears fell. Then a rush of my boys came back to me – anger, hurt, fear. Jesus, God, was there ever so much fear in them.

A pressure on the bed next to me and in a flurry I scrambled hard to get up; I couldn't let it happen again. He couldn't be back so fast. I made a quick run for the door.

Only ...

"Hank!" a deep familiar voice called out, stalling me from running further out of my room.

That voice. I knew that voice. I was five again and that voice echoed deep within me. A voice I missed more than anything.

Home ...
Hearth ...

Him.

And I smelled him. Christ on the mountain, did I ever smell him. I turned slowly to face him, not wanting to give into believing it could be true because I didn't think I could bear it if 'tweren't.

In an instant he took himself over the bed and scooped me up into his arms like I was just a little boy all over again.

His little boy.

"Hank, Jesus, son. My baby. My boy." Tears was flowing down his face as he kissed my forehead over and over, rocking me back and forth slowly. I breathed him in as the door to my bedroom burst open to reveal Mama and Cory standing there completely in shock. With a gasp my mother brought a hand up to her face, her eyes glistening as she saw the two of us.

"Cal?" She whispered softly to him. I kinda knew how she felt. It was like my nightmare had turned into the best fucking dream I could've had. Within the next few seconds, as if a curtain had been pulled back, I could feel my boys scrambling from across the town, trying to get their way back to me, their howls punctuating the night air, howls mixed with relief, tinged with fear. I knew they were coming.

My boys was comin'.

She came up to the both of us, her eyes wide with awe, as if she too thought she was dreaming all of this. Only I didn't have much in the way of sparin' a thought about that. I was too wrapped up in smelling him, feeling his love pour into me.

I had me my daddy again.

The one thing, the one part of me that never had a hope of being filled, of being complete, and now he was here, holding me so tight against him, his lips constantly kissing my forehead. I melted into him.

"I know I don't need to tell you two, but the boys are on their way," Cory said softly. "And Cal?"

I could feel him turn his attention her way but still not taking his lips from my forehead.

"They's gonna be plenty mad. They're gonna need your undivided attention. This here is a blood feud. No doubt about it. He was in the store today. Seems our Cade's gonna have himself a whole heap of trouble now."

Then she was gone. Where to I couldn't say.

My father lifted his lips from my forehead to answer; I missed him already. Years of needing this clawed at me – wanting him above all others. I was a grown man. But I would always be his little boy, the most special thing he'd ever done.

"You is magic personified ..." he once said to me many years ago as he tucked me in bed.

If I was, it was because my daddy was the most magical person who ever lived. And he saved me. There was no mistaking who had wrested me from that man's violation. My daddy had done that. He'd rescued me, like he always would.

"Let's get something set up for them 'cause the only way to calm a wolf down is by feedin' them. If anything, sweet coffee. I can get them talked down but I gotta get Hank sorted first." He leaned over and kissed my mama. I could sense them both still in love, still together even after all of this. I knew that there'd be a whole lotta talking but that would come later. I could hear voices downstairs.

My daddy turned back to me after placing a kiss on Mama's forehead.

"Go get him some pajama bottoms and a robe, will ya?"

Mama moved off, climbing over the debris in the room, which was sizable considering half the ceiling of my room was missing.

He walked us over to the bed and slowly sat down letting my legs rest across his lap. I didn't want to let go.

I know it was childish.

I know it was unbecoming of a young man to be so. But at this moment in time I wasn't a man. I was his boy. I needed to do some catching up now that he was back. Not that I had to relive my childhood – 'twasn't nothing like that. It was just that I needed a moment where it was just him and me, where I could bask in the love he had for me. I was starved for it, I was.

I was a boy who was approaching his eighteenth birthday in three days. A man by all rights, save one: I needed to be his boy just now. I needed my daddy in the worst way.

He kissed the side of my face and my forehead again. I curled into him as he rocked me slowly, whispering over and over, "'Sokay, I got you now. I got you now. I ain't ever gon' a let go. Never."

Then I heard him inside my head.

Son?

Yeah, Daddy?

I am so sorry I didn't get here faster. I didn't think he'd move as fast as he did. I nearly failed you, son. God almighty, that would've killed me. I can't lose ya. I just can't.

I felt the tears on his face as he nuzzled me back, my soft whimper to his low gravely growl.

'Salright. You came and you saved me. I ain't ever gonna forget that. But Daddy?

He spoke this time as Mama came upon us and handed me my pajama bottoms and I took them from her.

"What's that?" he said softly again as he let my feet swing out from his lap onto the floor so I could put the bottoms on. I quickly did so and leaned back into him. He pulled me to him and he was right: he wasn't ever gonna let me go now. I could tell.

"Why'd you have to leave us?"

He sighed and kissed my forehead again, letting his lips linger there and I closed my eyes and relished the feeling. All of the hurt and anguish of the past half hour leeched away in that soft caress of his lips. I could feel him pull it from me. A soft shudder coursed through him, eating away at the pain inside me, taking it in for himself, soothing what ailed.

Mama sat down next to him on the bed and for a moment, it was just the three of us – in the scattered debris of my room, splintered wood and plaster, the night sky twinkling above.

I could feel my boys pacing around downstairs. I knew Daddy could too. Somehow he was tied to all of us. And I knew we had to get down there soon or there'd be hell to pay. But I wanted my answer first. I needed to put that to bed.

"Well," he began softly, "there was just a point where I knew I was going to be too dangerous to be around you both. What I am attracts too much attention. Plus, we weren't too sure if what your Ma and me had done spared you from all of this. I didn't want this for you. I tried like hell to break you from it, Hank. Your mama and me wanted a normal life for you. We wanted you to be happy. But what we done, well, it unleashed something we weren't ready for. And it seemed instead of separating you from it, it only rooted itself even stronger. We misjudged the wolf."

He kissed my head again and I saw Mama lean her head onto Daddy's broad and powerful shoulder. He turned his head and kissed her for a moment before coming back to me.

"I am sorry I had to do that, but I was never far from you. I know you could smell me. It was my way of checking to see if you were free from it or not, and of my letting you know I was still around. I am sorry for letting you think I was gone. I am sorry for all of those empty years where I knew you needed me. Jesus, Hank, those were the hardest nights for me to bear. Many a night I'd sit in that tree right outside your window, watching over you, 'cause you are mine and I am yours. I ain't ever gonna set that down again. Ya hear? We'll figure it all out somehow. I swear it. But we'll do it together. As a family."

I nodded, a sniffle coming on me quick like. He chuckled and nuzzled me a bit more, before wrapping a powerful arm around Mama too.

I sat there for a moment and took them both in. My parents loved me quite a bit. I never doubted it. I didn't. Only I hadn't fully seen the enormity of it all until now. I was in awe of them both. And they were mine, and I was theirs.

We are a family.

We are one.

We are whole.

CHAPTER SEVEN

As With All Things ...

You can't imagine the oddest sight that confronted us when we came downstairs to find eight well-muscled and completely naked boys standing around, madder than fuck, with muscles rippling and a look of pure vengeance – angrier than a disturbed hornets' nest, they was. And there was no mistaking it: they were pissed because someone was trying to take what was theirs. They were visibly shaking with it.

That is, until they saw me.

Then like in a river rush of nothing but worry and so much fucking love they flooded my senses as Daddy carried me in his arms downstairs. It was silly of me, and I think Daddy might've thought so too if we both hadn't gone through what we had tonight. But there was just no way I was letting go of him right now and I think he knew that.

"Oh my word, boys. Now, I know you all can't run around in your wolf-form dressed but the very least Cory coulda done is break out some of Cal's old clothes for ya," Mama cried out as she descended quickly past us on the stairs and moved amongst the forest of muscle and bone what were my boys.

"And I am one step ahead a' ya," came Cory's reply with her arms full of shirts and pants from an old chest we had tucked away in the basement. They were a bit worn in but since Daddy was the biggest of them all – even if Tanner and Maynard were close seconds – we didn't have to worry none about them not fitting my boys. 'Twere baggy on a few of them but they'd do. Some of the boys just shucked into the pants Cory'd offered them and then only cursorily slipped into a flannel shirt without bothering to button up. Jesus, were they ever the most beautiful sight I'd ever seen. *My boys.*

And they were, too. I could feel them. They was still *all mine.*

Tanner and Riley just grabbed pants, not bothering with a shirt. They were all watching me outta the corner of their eyes as Daddy retook his chair at the head of the table with me still in his lap. I had taken to putting my head on his shoulder in the crook of his neck, taking long drawing breaths, breathing him in so deeply. It seemed to soothe my soul. With each inhalation his hand would gently but purposefully stroke the back of my head. No longer that faint whisper of him along the breeze, this was real. It was all him I was breathing in and he just kept running a soothing hand along the back of my head with a deep purr in his chest.

I was his and he was mine.

Father and son.

Each time I thought that, he'd rumble in agreement and I could feel him moving within me. He flooded me with such a possessive love that it was staggering. I trembled a bit from it all. My daddy was a truly awesome thing to behold.

Riley and Tanner were on us first, each one moving in quiet-like. I silently watched them as they approached my father: it was clear who was the real Alpha in this house. And Daddy was putting out a strong signal that no one better think of reaching for me just yet.

Riley and Tanner took up the same chairs as they had only a few hours ago, only turning them to face inward. I sorta marveled at how so much had changed in the span of those few hours. Daddy just eyed them for a moment.

I felt I needed to say something to him. I gently reached out to him to see how he was feeling about it all. While I could feel him pouring into me, he was something of a mystery. The link didn't seem to flow as easily up that shared stream.

You okay with this, Daddy? I didn't ask for any of it. It just sorta happened. Riley said it was destiny or somethin'. I don't rightly know if 'tis or not. But they said you had a part in of them bein' who they are. I guess I shoulda been payin' more attention to that. 'Cause they'd only turned a few years ago it seems, so the only way that coulda happened was if you were still alive. I can see that now.

He just kept rubbing his hand along the back of my head and I was the happiest boy I coulda ever been. I didn't want it to end. But my boys needed me. I knew they did. They was scared that something had been broken, and very nearly 'twas. I was sure by now that my daddy's legs were going all numb from me being so danged big and all.

I pulled away from the comfort of his neck and looked at him. I pressed my forehead against his and I felt his breath come out slow and soft, billowing across my face. I breathed him in and it was just like I was five again. It was just him and me.

Only 'twasn't, not really, not anymore.

I heard his voice rumble inside of me, and not just my head neither.

He was truly in every part of me, stronger than my boys ever were. This was his blood, his bones, his heart that was beating right along with my own. His eyes slowly opened and my bright blues was staring right back into his.

"You let me talk to the boys for a bit, okay? Then you can go down and get cleaned up with them. They need to be with ya in that way, Hank." He gave me a look that said he was just fine with how things were. I nodded even if I felt my body go tense at the thought of sex.

He shushed me and brushed the bangs from across my forehead and continued, "Not like Cade, Hank. You *know* it ain't ever gonna be like Cade was. He needed magic to do what he done. You didn't have a say, now didja?"

I wanted to tell him about that small tiny, but powerful seed that had started to take root in me during Cade's forcing himself on me, but I thought better of it. So I shrugged and nodded that he had the right of it.

"Now, you take a good long look at your boys, 'cause they's yours now, and you know they is, don'tcha?" I just sat there. I could feel all of them on tenterhooks just waiting for me to deny them. But I wouldn't. I couldn't. It just wasn't in me. But I was still sort of embarrassed and ashamed for what I'd let happen to me. So I didn't know how to respond. I didn't know what to say to them all.

"Well, go on and look at them," he nudged with his chin in their direction. Now fully clothed, they all collected around the large table again.

So look, I did. I turned my head slowly, my eyes to the table. I could feel them along that link we all shared. But I was afraid of what they'd see in me. But Daddy said to look, and I had to trust that. He'd never steer me wrong. Never.

My eyes slowly moved to meet their gaze. All I could feel was love and concern for me. They seemed to know what almost happened tonight. They seemed to understand that while Mama and Cory had done their level best to bind me to them as much as they could, Cade had anticipated their every move.

His words came back to me just then, and I shuttered them against my boys as much as I could. It seemed to work even if those words were like a venom moving around inside.

Hank, you is mine now. Don't bother tryin' to fight this. I'm too strong for you to overcome. You can thank your daddy for that, too. He was my lover for many years and taught me so much. I realize it was what could bring you to me now. Your daddy was just the practice for you comin' into my world. I sees that now. Time to claim what's rightfully mine.

As that thought moved across my mind I could see that each of my boys was getting a clearer picture of just how close we all came to having what we were building come to nothing. Worse yet, it woulda irretrievably destroyed my boys. That thought was crushing to me. I couldn't imagine a world without them now.

But they heard me think about Cade's words as he forced his way onto me, even if they didn't know what was said – *in* me. That was the part that brought about shame. That was the part I felt I'd failed them all.

It was Riley's voice that reached me first.

"We could never be ashamed of you, Hank. Can't you see how much we all love you? Can't you feel it none?"

I nodded, unable to say anything, angry for not being a stronger man, for not knowing how to take Cade on in his own game.

"Babe?" I felt Riley's hand under my chin, a gentle finger lifting my eyes to meet his. "Nothing is ever gonna take you away from us, Hank O'Malley. We belong to you now, 'member?"

A single tear escaped from my face. He leaned down and kissed my forehead. His lips were so soft, like an angel himself was blessing me or something, that's the only way I can describe it. It was heavenly.

Daddy nudged me with his right hand along my thigh. He wanted to get up as Mama and Cory brought cups and some coffee to the table for the boys. There was also a heaping bowl of sugar too, 'cause it seemed my boys had one helluva sweet tooth and somehow Cory seemed to know this. A tall plate of black currant and maple bacon scones was placed on the table too. They didn't last long.

I got up and moved to Riley's lap instead. It was weak of me but I needed contact with someone I could love who could love me back. I still felt incredibly violated. There was a part of me that realized that in the middle of it all, I'd actually began to enjoy what Cade was doing to me. Not emotionally, 'cause I didn't have any kind of attachment to the man in that way. But my body seemed to respond to being fucked like I was, like it had a mind of its own and didn't much care who was doing the fucking.

It didn't matter. But despite my body's traitorous response, I did mind who was doing it. A resolve began to form. Riley ran a finger under my chin and brought my lips to his so softly. Small chaste kisses, pouring himself into my heart, doing what he thought he could to heal me.

Daddy eyed us for a second before he smirked and turned to the boys. Only whatever had made him smile at what was going on between Riley and me faded and he became deadly serious, so much so that it put an abrupt stop to Riley's healing ways.

"Now that I am back, word's gonna travel and it won't be pretty. There's a blood feud on now, with a pack lover I had who I foolishly showed what I could do. He ain't got nothin' but parlor tricks between what Ruth, Cory and I can do. But we aren't even close to the power that I put into play with you boys and Hank. I am sorry, but I woulda liked it if you all progressed like I thought you would – discoverin' one another and what Hank means to you all, and all of it, in your own good time. It's what I truly wanted for ya. I did."

He leaned forward, resting his large hands onto the table top, ensuring that every eye at this table was on him. There was no doubt they 'twere.

I could feel Daddy move amongst us, on the inside. Where me and my boys was like a powerful creek, Daddy was a river, broad and incredibly powerful. Feeling him like that was the best salve to soothe what was ailing me. I could tell he was doing it to give my boys some needed focus. I could tell he knew that without it, they were gonna leave here tonight hell-bent on revenge. I could tell that that would be the worst way to deal with the likes of Cade. Daddy may have said he only had parlor tricks, but there was a part of me that knew that wasn't wholly true. What Cade had accomplished that no one wanted to admit, including myself, was that he was strong enough not only to keep me pinned down and compliant, but he'd gotten into a house with two powerful witches who lived with me. Not to mention he knew enough to slip past my daddy who said he was watching over me. So inwardly, tucking it into the blackest of my thoughts, I buried that little bit of information. Something wasn't quite clicking into place. Daddy's words brought me out of my darker thoughts.

"Now, that isn't to say that Cade Bowen is a flit you can toss to the road, either. He's crafty. I knew he was crafty when he first came to me in the pack I was in with Cory's husband. I knew Cade was gunning for me from the moment I joined the pack. He wanted me because he had designs on being an Alpha of his own pack. Cade craves one thing above all else: power. And he knew that I could give that to him."

He stood up straight and I spied the taut muscled body my daddy possessed – Jesus, even now, thirteen years older than I recalled, was he ever a sight to behold. In that moment I wanted to be just like him. He scratched the back of his head as he seemed to struggle with saying the next part.

"Only, while I say that he has parlor tricks up his sleeve he does have an ace, and it's a fairly big 'un, too: *allure*. He's got heaps and heaps of it. He could bed any one of us within a matter of seconds, despite our resolve, despite any knowledge we had about him before we run into him. When he talks, your mind gets all clouded and suddenly all you can hear is him. It's his strongest suit because of our need to be with our kind in that way. It's an exchange of power, you see. But I know I don't need to tell you all that. We went through that together when I turned each of you. So you know what that is like, right? You remember it?"

They all looked at one another and small bursts of them being with my daddy in that way suddenly started to pop into my mind. It was strange to see my daddy with these boys but I could tell that sex with them was part of the binding. Which meant ...

"Yeah, babe, your Daddy's our Alpha. But he built this pack for you, on account of who and what you are," Riley whispered to me.

At this point Tanner seemed to have enough of being on the other side of us so he got up and gently padded his way to where I was with Riley. He leaned forward and kissed me softly for a second or two, pouring some of himself back into me with that kiss.

He knelt down beside us and the fingers of his big right hand laced with mine. They both needed to touch me, and I realized just how much I needed them, too. It was helping me, leeching the shame of Cade's heinous attack from me. It was becoming distant, lesser. Not forgotten, because I knew that'd be too dangerous, given what Daddy'd said about it all. No, I realized we all needed to remember the likes of Cade Bowen and just what he was capable of.

"It don't matter what bindings you have, 'cause I know. I was pledged to Cory's husband through and through; didn't matter a heap when Cade had me alone. And he made plenty sure he got me alone whenever he could. I couldn't think. I couldn't push back. The only way I can deal with Cade is to surprise him like I did tonight. He can't see or smell me comin' or he'll direct hisself at me and I go all foggy. He knows how to fuck with your head; he plays to our wolf instincts. And he's good at it, very, *very,* good at it. Y'all need to remember that. Got it?"

They all looked amongst each other before nodding as they sipped their coffee some and chewed the last of their scones.

He nodded that he got through what he wanted them all to hear.

"Now, Ruth, Cory and I are going to ward the house. He won't be able to get through that. Those of you who need to get back home tonight then just do so now 'cause what we put into play will have to stay up until dawn. With that gapin' hole in Hank's bedroom the only thing that will keep us all safe is to ward the area. So, while we do that, why don't you all take Hank downstairs and get reacquainted with each other. I know you all need it and Hank needs it most of all."

He glanced back at me, his eyes soft and wide as he drank me in. That strong current of love he had for me came at a rush inside of me. I felt myself flush with it. But I didn't try to do anything but drink him in. I know they all said in one way or another that Daddy had built all of this for me, that somehow I was key to it all. Only with him here, it was clear that I had quite a bit of making up lost time to do. I had to listen to what Daddy told me, trust in what he had to say was what was best. I knew that might sound like I was weak but I knew 'twasn't like that a'tall.

Daddy was stepping up so he could train me on what I was here to do. And that had something to do with whatever it was that I was. *Which was ...*

"An Omega," Tanner answered softly in my direction.

Daddy just nodded once. I could tell there was more to the story but I'd have to wait on that one a bit.

He turned back to the boys. "We can pick this up in the morning. Don't know if you all will be makin' it to school tomorrow. Is that going to be a problem?"

The boys shook their heads in unison. It seemed whatever was going to go down they weren't going anywhere without me.

Daddy nodded.

"Well, get Hank downstairs and you boys see to him. It won't be the Binding 'cause that can't happen for another two days yet, but he needs you powerfully strong even though he hasn't realized it yet. I know what I speak of."

I glanced at Mama, knowing hearing all of this wolf pack talk couldn't be easy for her none. It wasn't but she was bearing it. That life of hers bound with him was already on the road to becoming familiar again. But there was a tremendous amount of love and pride she had in us. Even I could see that through all of the mess that Cade had visited on us tonight.

With that, the boys finished drinking their coffee and wiped their mouths with the backs of their sleeves. Riley began to stand up, bringing me up in his arms with him. It wasn't that I couldn't walk. I knew I could. I wasn't damaged in any real way, other than I really felt the need to touch them. Maybe this was what Daddy meant by my needing them.

Riley then handed me off to Tanner which sorta surprised me, but that was because he stopped to talk to my daddy while Tanner followed the boys down the stairs to the basement. I spied my father and Riley speaking very animatedly at each other. I tried to listen in along our link but I found I couldn't. It seemed Daddy was doing the blocking this time around. I'd have to remember that too.

Tanner pulled focus as we descended the stairs, his face nuzzling into my neck, licking and kissing it tenderly. His face was wet with a few tears 'cause I could feel how upset he was inside. As soon as the boys reached the basement, the clothes began to come off. Riley had joined us by now, a look of defiance and determination about him that wasn't there before. I tried to sneak a small peek into his mind but there was no reaching him there. Not that he wasn't letting me in, there just seemed to be a "locked door" that I couldn't breach no matter how much I tried.

The lights flickered and there was a low hum coming at us from all sides. I sorta panicked 'cause I didn't know what was going on.

"It's the wards. Natural magic always seems to cause havoc with the mundane world. It's just what they said they was gonna do," Ry offered.

I nodded once but didn't find a whole lot of comfort in it. Secrets, there seemed to be more secrets here than before. Locked doors, shut out communication, a whole bunch of ways I could see things shift for us. I didn't like it.

"No one does," Riley said as he finished shucking himself out of his pants to let all the gloriousness of him be exposed to the world. And he was glorious. All of my boys were. I watched them all as they approached me and Tanner. Tanner just wrapped his big arms around my front, keeping my back to him but never so far as to be constricting. More of just letting me know he had my back.

Mike was at the shower starting it up and getting the water hot. The other boys started to move over to it but sorta lined up the path to where Mike had it all ready, spindles of steam spiraling up the sides. He looked very sexy under the stream of water. Thank God Daddy built the shower stall as large as he did. I guess he wanted the space or ... Wow, it suddenly occurred to me that he built it for this very reason that I was about to use it for.

That thought had my head spinning that my daddy and I shared that peculiar aspect of our lives.

Things was all gaummed up, that's for damned sure.

But my boys were standing there, naked, looking so fucking beautiful that my heart hurt for each of them. I almost lost them all. They almost slipped away.

I knew it wasn't over. I knew that my boys were needing me, wanting to spend that moment where I would give myself to each of them, allowing them to heal me as much as my near miss of losing them all needed healing in them too.

I stood at the entrance to the shower.

"C'mon in. The water's nice and hot. Just like me," Mike said with a wicked wiggle of his brows. I smiled softly at him in turn and was pleased at how hard I was making him watching me remove my PJ's as my boys came around to pass them from me onto some feed sacks that were stacked down a piece beyond the shower area. Toby laid them all out nice and neat for me for when I was done.

I noted that there was a bevy of towels already laid out for us. Cory was nothing if not thorough. I had to give her that. Actually, as I moved from being slightly embarrassed to be amongst my boys while my newly reunited family was putting up magical protections around us, with the lights flickering every now and again, I felt my body pull upon my boys. I felt the incredible wave of love and attention they wanted to give me.

I had me eight boyfriends.

I had me a pack.

And I was loved – by all of them. The center of their love, actually. My boys pressed in upon me. Kisses both deep and chaste, hands roaming and touching me, pulling upon my heart with each caress. Mouths enveloping parts of me, my boys each in turn probing me, feeling the length and immensity of them as they poured every bit of themselves on me. It was towering; it was monumental, an ocean of feelings they had for me, shaking me to my core. I shuddered with their attentions, realizing I almost lost this. I almost succumbed to it all being torn away from me.

And yet, as I felt lips and hands and hearts from every direction assault my senses to where I couldn't think straight, I realized one other dark thing. One thing that had taken root while Cade had fucked me relentlessly. One word that still haunted me from the first time I heard it uttered in the throes of my orgasm with Riley earlier.

It was that word that chilled me to my core, but I hid it. I protected it from my boys, because me and my boys was going to war. I didn't know if we were to survive it at all. So I gave of myself willingly to them. I wanted them all to have some part of me that was theirs. But that icy point, that singular word gnawed at me. It took root and festered, unabated and evil. And it had a voice, and that voice had a name now: Cade Bowen.

And *he* said ...

Soon.

CHAPTER EIGHT

Epilogue - A Rising In The North

Moving within that boy was the best fucking feeling a man could have, like a drug or the best damned moonshine you'd ever taste: the slow burn that made you want to beg for more. What his body could do to a man ... well, there just weren't any women that could do that. I could draw on him like I was siphoning gas from a truck, suck that power right out of him and he had no way of knowing what I was up to.

And Lord, was he ever a wellspring of power, like the deepest pool of it without end. Fucking him was like dipping my wick into raw unbridled power. Those boys just don't know what they've got.

And I intend on keeping it that way, too.

But one thing was sure: what those boys had been saying about him wasn't a stretch of the imagination or nothing. He was the real thing.

Magic, pure and simple. Raw, powerful and *such* a good lay too. I could fuck that boy into oblivion and he'd love every second of it and beg for more. I could juice up on that boy for days and never want to stop.

But I had a plan.

I had it all laid out. I knew just when their guard would be down. I spied it in them, saw their weaknesses, chief amongst them was their arrogance that they had it all in the bag.

Shit, stupid-assed fuckers. They weren't ready for the likes of me, that's for sure.

I took another swig from the glass of fine whiskey I'd acquired in Nashville a few weeks back. Cal had no idea what I'd become since he disappeared. Died in the war they said. Saw his wife and that sweet little boy of Cal's at the small gravestone they put up for him in the cemetery. Nothing to bury as he'd died across the seas and the body had never been recovered.

Without Cal around there didn't seem to be much for me in Sparrows. Not like there ever was.

I scratched my balls as they'd never had the chance to seed the boy properly. I hadn't bothered with redressing myself – it was just me in the house now anyway. My domain, my pack, and my rules. That's how it worked now. I got up and looked out over the city of Charleston. I'd made a name for myself in those intervening years while I waited for Hank to grow up. Always kept my nose to the wind in those parts. Hunted there. Spied on the boy and waited for the time when his musk would change and I knew he'd be ripe for the plucking.

And pluck I did – or tried to, at any rate. I didn't expect the outcome. That was for sure.

Yet, something had seen to that. It wasn't his witch of a mother nor Cory that'd put a stop to it, that's for sure. No, someone else was at work in that moment. Someone familiar to who and what I'd become had wrenched me away from my prize – and I was so close to breeding myself into him and imprinting myself irrevocably in him.

I should've just fucked him brutally 'til the deed was done. I chastised myself.

But I was too caught up myself in what he was. There was a danger threaded through what I had in Hank. He was powerful all right, of that I had no doubt. But I also knew it was unwieldy too. I didn't think I could ever truly master him. He'd be like cuddling with a copperhead. Where Cal had been the consummate lover, and if his wife wasn't in the picture, I'd dare say mate, he was never going to submit to being with me in that way, despite how well we worked together.

At times, like now, full of drink and feeling a bit battered, I missed the fuck out of Cal.

"Stop your blubbering ..." I grimaced against those lustful thoughts and drank the last of the whiskey in the tumbler. Its warmth needled its way down into my belly, making the pang of not getting Hank like I wanted tonight to lessen the tiniest bit.

"Is it done?" a deep bass voice rumbled from the darkness of the room as I stood against the large window looking over the city below. I didn't care much who saw me. I had enough money to keep things quiet. Yes, those years I spent away from Hank O'Malley were well-spent years, allowed me to reinvent myself and become quite powerful in my own right. That allure trick that Cal had shown me had proven more than its worth, allowing me to escape my hillbilly ways and establish myself as an upstanding community member after years of toiling and accumulating power in New York. They didn't know me as Cade Bowen but as Cade Talbot. It was my mother's maiden name but it was enough to fully separate me from my poorer past.

I walked away from the window and poured another glass of whiskey.

I wanted to get truly fucked up tonight. I knew I couldn't go back just yet. They'd be expecting that. I needed to bide my time, to see when the next crack in their armor would form, something I could exploit. From the looks of it that McGhee boy was just the sort of target I could work on. He seemed to want to rattle the cages around Riley's pack. He could just be what I needed to unhinge them all.

"No, I didn't get to finish what I started." I swallowed the entire tumbler in one big swig, loving the bite it took out of me as it went down.

"So, I take it he's not one of us then?"

I threw the fucking tumbler across the room and it smashed into the wall, embedding most of it there in a smattering of glittering glass with what little light was coming through the windows. It gleamed in the moonlight.

"No! He is NOT one of the pack, Marcus! Something just ... got in the way."

His dark-skinned arms slinked around my waist; his hands roaming down to grip my cock and balls with absolute authority. As my beta it was his turf and he knew it. When I was pissed and needed some bringing down, he knew sex was the best way to do that. I couldn't blame him. He was just running to what had worked before.

I gave into his strong caresses for a moment before I pulled from his embrace.

"Go get into bed. I'll be there in a few."

I could hear him debate my words for a moment before he gently padded off to our room down the long hallway before my voice stalled him in his tracks.

"And Marcus," I said over my shoulder as I approached the shards of glass in the wall looking like I imagined encrusted diamonds in a mine might look. I heard him stop.

"Get out the cuffs. I'm gonna be particularly brutal tonight. I need to work something out in my head — you know how that goes."

Marcus smiled darkly. He had a particular penchant for being rough during sex.

"Do you require a third?" he asked softly, his voice so deep and dark that I grew hard just hearing him, a stream of pre-cum already dripping from my tip of my cock.

"Yes, why don't you?" I started to gently run a tentative finger over the sharp angles of the tumbler in the wall, never pressing so hard that they cut me.

"See if Timmy is available. He likes it when I play hard."

Marcus tilted his head slightly because he recalled the last time I nearly mauled the boy and he still came back for more. He was a very pliant boy to plunder when I was angry.

He slowly departed. I could hear his bare feet moving softly on the wooden floor several feet away – receding, getting things ready.

"What could've taken me by surprise like that, I wonder?" I murmured aloud, unsure of what it could be.

No one had ever taken me by surprise like that, not in all the years I'd been plying my magical talents. No one except Cal, that is. But he was dead so there just wasn't any way that ...

"No body to bury ..." I murmured to myself.

My eyes widened with that thought and I realized the game had just changed. I moved off down the hall, a plan already forming in my head, a dark and malicious plan on how I'd have not only the son, but the father as well. A wickedly delicious smile snaked across my lips, my cock lengthening for the grueling fuck that was to come, how I'd violate Marcus and Timmy eight ways come Sunday while working out the kinks in my newly formed plan. I had only one word percolating on my mind.

It bubbled and boiled forth, oozing over my whiskey tinged lips.

Father *and* son.

"Soon ... "

www.ingramcontent.com/pod-product-compliance
Lightning Source LLC
Chambersburg PA
CBHW060149130626
46556CB00006B/2554